"My father's betrayal of your family was not something I had any idea of."

"And I have no designs to blame you for it. You were a mere child."

"So were you."

Cairo regarded Ariel for a long moment. He had not felt like a child. Not since he had escaped the palace that day. He had known then that all he could do was survive. He'd had to. For he was the only remaining living member of his family who was not being held in captivity. Survival was not an option. It was a directive.

"Then you aren't here for revenge?"

Revenge would be a much simpler task. Revenge he'd taken already, and it had been easy, cathartic.

Ariel had never been easy for him.

But atonement required sacrifice.

And she was that.

"No. I'm here to ensure that the contract is honored. My brother has been freed, and he needs a wife."

"I don't suppose there's any chance of you trying to find another one."

"No. There is not. You were promised to my family, and my family has lost too much of what it is owed. I will not see this ended as well."

The Royal Desert Legacy

Claiming the throne...and their brides!

The lives of teenage princes Cairo and Riyaz changed forever the day their parents were killed in a violent coup. Cairo escaped, but the heir to the throne, Riyaz, was mercilessly imprisoned.

Now, years later, Riyaz is finally free and it's time for him to take his rightful place as the leader of Nazul, with his brother by his side! Yet two women are about to throw their carefully constructed plans for justice into disarray...

Cairo must return his brother's promised bride, Ariel, to Nazul. Except their own childhood friendship has become something so much more electric...and dangerous!

Read Cairo and Ariel's story in
Forbidden to the Desert Prince

Available now!

As Riyaz learns how to navigate royal life again, there's only one woman the sheikh wants. And it's not the one he's supposed to marry!

Look for Riyaz and Brianna's story

Coming soon!

Maisey Yates

FORBIDDEN TO THE
DESERT PRINCE

Recycling programs
for this product may
not exist in your area.

ISBN-13: 978-1-335-58397-0

Forbidden to the Desert Prince

Copyright © 2022 by Maisey Yates

Harlequin Enterprises ULC
22 Adelaide St. West, 41st Floor
Toronto, Ontario M5H 4E3, Canada
www.Harlequin.com

Printed in U.S.A.

Maisey Yates is a *New York Times* bestselling author of over one hundred romance novels. Whether she's writing strong, hardworking cowboys, dissolute princes or multigenerational family stories, she loves getting lost in fictional worlds. An avid knitter with a dangerous yarn addiction and an aversion to housework, Maisey lives with her husband and three kids in rural Oregon. Check out her website, maiseyyates.com.

Books by Maisey Yates

Harlequin Presents

His Forbidden Pregnant Princess
Crowned for My Royal Baby
The Secret That Shocked Cinderella

Pregnant Princesses

Crowned for His Christmas Baby

The Heirs of Liri

His Majesty's Forbidden Temptation
A Bride for the Lost King

Visit the Author Profile page
at Harlequin.com for more titles.

For the readers, you're why these books exist,
and I'm so thankful.

CHAPTER ONE

Run.

ARIEL HART STARED at the text message on her phone. For just one breath.

Then she sprang into action. She had known this moment could come. She'd known to be prepared for it.

"Darling," her mother had tried to reassure her, *"he's been imprisoned for years. He may have died in captivity. You don't know if he'll come for you."*

But she *had* known.

Her father had meddled in affairs he never should have and he'd used her as a chess piece and…

No time for self-pity, Ari, get it together.

She changed her clothing, quickly, taking off the cashmere sweatpants and equally soft cable-knit sweater she was wearing, trading them out for a pair of black leggings and a black hoodie that felt stiff as cardboard. She put the hood up over her white-blond hair and tucked each strand beneath it. She slipped on a pair of black trainers, picked up her black duffel bag and looked around her beautiful Parisian apartment one last time.

She'd felt safe here.

It was tranquil. Beautiful. All pale pinks and soothing tans. That she now looked like a cat burglar seemed an affront to the subtlety of the space.

She'd made a life here. Started her career.

For years she'd lived looking over her shoulder. Moving all the time, using assumed names. But about seven years after she'd… stopped. It was in the back of her mind that it could happen, she still had a go bag. But it had seemed unlikely. She didn't know if Riyaz was alive. She didn't know if Cairo was alive.

That was one reason she and her mother had taken it on themselves to simply…be wary. How could you call the police or an embassy about a potential threat from another country by persons who had not threatened you, in all actuality, and might in fact be dead?

But in her heart she'd known.

That he could come for her in search of revenge, or marriage.

And she didn't want either.

She'd leave it all behind now.

She'd be a fugitive, not a fashion designer.

But there was no space for pity. Not now.

It was possibly a matter of life and death, and there was no time to feel sorry for herself in the face of that.

She'd felt sorry for herself twenty years ago when she'd discovered—at age eight—that her father had promised her to a stranger. She'd felt sorry for herself, wandering the glittering halls at the palace in Nazul, looking at all the glorious mosaics and sitting by the fountains, the scent of orange blossom in the arid desert air.

And when her father had used the access he'd gained to the palace to assist in a coup that overthrew the royal family of Nazul and left the sheikh and sheikha dead, one son thrown into a dungeon and the other...

Missing.

Cairo.

She didn't think of him often, or at least, she tried not to.

The younger brother, the one with a ready smile and engaging dark eyes, so unlike the one she was promised to marry. The boy who had become her friend. Her confidant. Her first heartbreak.

When she was thirteen, she'd been sitting in the courtyard one day, baking in the sun and sulking, and there he'd been.

"Not enjoying yourself, ya amar?"

"It's very hot."

"It is the desert."

"I want to go back to Europe. I hate it here."

"Europe? You're American, Ari, are you not?"

"We spend half the year in Paris."

"Ah, how very nice."

"Nicer than this."

"Tell me, are you angry at this place? Or at its intent for you?"

"It's all the same."

"I don't think that's true. If you look around you might see that the place and the purpose are not one in the same. And perhaps...you might enjoy aspects of your time here."

And then he'd reached up and picked an orange from the tree above and handed it to her.

"Whether you wish to like it or not, the trees yet grow fruit. It cannot be all bad. Think on that, ya amar.*"*

My moon. He had called her that for some reason she had never been able to figure out.

He said it as if to mock her and yet she'd always felt such an odd tangle inside her when he said things like that.

Cairo had been the closest thing to joy on those trips to Nazul. Though it had gotten thorny and complicated when she was twelve, and he thirteen, and he had suddenly grown very tall, and she'd found it hard to speak to him.

It had been such a funny thing. One year she'd gone to visit and they'd run around the palace like wild, feral things like they had since she was eight. And the next…she'd been shy around him. They'd had one whole year of barely speaking.

But that day she hadn't hidden from him. That day, he'd given her an orange.

And from there something else had blossomed between them. Something tender and precious and aching. She thought she might be in love, and she knew it was impossible. After five days she'd gone back to Paris. And the day after that…

The world had ended. At least in Nazul.

The heir, her fiancé, Riyaz was taken prisoner. Held as collateral.

And Cairo?

He had either been killed along with palace resisters, his body discarded as if he were nothing, not even important enough to be identified.

Or he had disappeared.

It didn't matter now. Riyaz was out. And that meant…

He would either seek to claim his bride or his revenge, and she wanted no part of either.

The sins of her father were his to pay, not hers.

But she would still have to face consequences.

She put on her backpack and headed to the door, and opened it.

And stopped.

He was there.

Standing there. Taller, broader and just plain more than when last she'd seen him. It wasn't Riyaz, or a cavalcade of soldiers, like she'd seen in her nightmares. It wasn't the monster she had trained herself to fear, to run from.

It was *him.*

Cairo al Hadid.

Very much alive.

And in her hallway.

"Ya amar," he said. "I have come for you."

Sheikh Cairo Ahmad Syed al Hadid had been a man without a country for far too long.

Perhaps that was not an accurate portrayal of the situation. He had a country. And he had not forgotten. He had made it his mission to take down the invading forces. All these years, he had not forgotten. The screams of his mother. The dying bellow of his father as he took his sword and did battle, though it was futile. Because he was King of Nazul, and he would have never let it fall without a fight. And it would never have fallen if not for the betrayal.

A betrayal at the hands of the Hart patriarch. Dominic Hart had gotten greedy. He had taken his connection to the royal family of Nazul, and he had decided instead to take the money of a vicious warlord in order to betray the al Hadid family.

The man had been an Eastern European mercenary who'd decided he was done running missions and gaining power for others, and had decided to take power where he could for himself. He'd chosen Nazul because it was rich in natural resources, and small enough, with few enough allies on a global scale that he would face few consequences for his actions.

But Cairo had seen that there were consequences. That man had been on the throne these past years, and Cairo had taken great joy in ending his reign. In watching his face when Cairo and his army for hire had stormed the palace and he'd known.

He'd known.

Cairo was not there to take prisoners.

Bloody battles had a cost. Revenge had a cost.

But Cairo owed that debt. He still owed a debt.

His life, his desires, his body, his soul. They were not his own. He'd lost his right to a life that belonged to himself all those years ago on a desert night when he'd made a mistake that had cost everything.

And so he'd lived these past years knowing this moment would come, and that when it did, he would give all to see his country restored.

To his brother sitting on the throne, as the rightful leader of Nazul.

He'd escaped the palace that day.

But he'd known he would return.

He had moved to England and begun using the name Syed al Shahar, his mother's family name. He had used his wit and his understanding of systems to get himself into the finest schools on scholarship. From there, he had begun to build an empire.

And people might know Cairo as a playboy, businessman and mogul, but they did not know that he had been a boy who had watched his family die in a palace in a far-off desert kingdom that made few headlines.

What was yet more global unrest, after all? It had been a blip on the radar of the news media in Europe and the United States, for what did they care? People killing each other in a country that none of them wanted to visit anyway.

That was how they ranked their concern. Did they wish to vacation there? Or was the country in question potentially going to invade them? If not… A cruel footnote in the history of a world filled with cruel histories. Unremarkable. And yet, it had changed his entire life.

He had known, though.

He had *known* that Riyaz had survived. He had felt that in his bones. Either way, Cairo's loyalty was to Nazul. And he had built his empire on the foundation of wanting nothing more than to destroy the men that had killed his family. That had taken his legacy.

And he had known that if his brother truly were being held captive, then he must be rescued. Cairo would always come for him.

He might be Syed to the world, but he had always been Cairo.

Always.

He knew what he had to do. All the parties, all the excess…it was never for him. And if it successfully helped to burn away the memories of what had happened in Nazul?

He did not mind having those memories blurred.

He didn't need them sharp to fulfill his mission.

He knew who he was. He might have indulged himself in the pleasures to be found in the world. It had started as a way to gain access to parties and by extension, to people.

But he found that he had an endless capacity to work hard, and to pursue divine degradation even harder.

And so he had built himself an empire. One that allowed him to move freely between nations. Collect allies and data, and many other things that aided him in this overthrow of the overthrowers.

He'd also found himself in many rooms with men who were dangerous and lacked scruples. He'd saved a girl from one of those rooms.

Brianna Whitman.

He'd helped her escape the fate set out for her by her father, sent her to school, and she'd become an accomplished life coach for people who had come from difficult circumstances, and while he found all of that to be modern, soft nonsense…

It had seemed less nonsensical when he saw his brother for the first time in fifteen years. He'd hired Brianna then, to go and try to help him. Coax him back to the world, to the position of his birth. She was there now, trying her best to help him become the man he was meant to be, rather than the beast he'd been fashioned into through years of isolation.

Riyaz was free. But Riyaz was not… He was certainly not fit to rule. He was blunt and he lacked even basic manners. He had spent the years in the dungeon reading and honing his body into a war machine. He was a strange mix of things, his brother. Well-read, for he'd had nothing to do in the dungeon but read, and he'd done so to keep his language alive. He had also worked out exhaustively to avoid letting any part of him atrophy.

But he had no practice of applying these things in the real world. He could hardly hold a conversation, let alone engage in matters of global diplomacy.

Cairo's taking of the palace in Nazul was a secret. To the nation, to the world. They'd power, but they continued to operate in stealth mode, particularly as he figured out when he could present Riyaz to the people.

They would have only one chance to do so.

Riyaz could not be seen as weak mentally. He could not be seen as affected by what he'd endured. The people would want a strong, triumphant return.

When Riyaz had been freed from the dungeon, Cairo had been there.

His brother had been dressed in near rags, his hair and beard long. Cairo had expected to find him weak and pale, but Riyaz had been built of pure muscle and rage. He refused to go outside. He refused to sleep in a bed. He spent much of his time in the dungeon still.

He had asked for two things upon his freedom.

A cheeseburger, and Ariel Hart.

Ariel...

The name had been a jagged, whispered memory to Cairo.

But he had known just where she was.

He had always known.

He had thought of going to her, many times. And yet he'd known there was only ever one circumstance under which he could see her again. If Riyaz wanted her.

And Riyaz wanted her.

So Cairo would do what Riyaz had asked. He owed him that.

"You had to know that I would come for you," he said.

"I…"

She was beautiful. She was orange blossoms in a mosaic garden that he had not seen in more than a decade. She was rich, perfumed air. She was a moment in time he could never have back.

It was the impact of her that shocked him. For Cairo was dead to most things in the world. He felt rage, and he felt desire, he had felt something larger than himself when Riyaz had been freed from the dungeon.

But this… Her… She was incredibly beautiful. She surpassed that which she had promised to become. For she had always been lovely.

Her robin's egg blue eyes were wide as she looked up at him. She was dressed as if she was ready to run. She had been warned.

"Are you here to kill me?" she whispered.

"No," he said. "That would be far too basic, and I am a civilized man."

"And not dead," she pointed out.

"No. At least not last I checked." He looked at her yet more intently. "Did you think that I was?"

"I did not discount it." She looked away, and he was certain he saw regret in her eyes, sadness. But he was not swayed by it. "I know the fate of the rest of your family."

"Riyaz lives."

She nodded slowly. "Is that why you're here? Because of Riyaz?"

"Yes," said Cairo. "I am here on behalf of my brother. You don't seem shocked that Riyaz is alive."

"There were rumors. That he had been kept alive and imprisoned in the palace. Collateral of some kind. I do not fully understand."

"Neither do I. But can one understand the will of a madman? Your father is included in that."

"My father's betrayal of your family was not something I had any idea of."

"And I have no designs to blame you for it. You were a mere child."

"So were you."

He regarded her for a long moment. He had not felt like a child. Not since he had escaped the palace that day. He had known then that all he could do was survive. He'd had to. For he was the only remaining, living member of his family that was not being held in captivity. Survival was not an option. It was a directive.

"Then, you aren't here for revenge?"

Revenge would be a much simpler task. Revenge he'd taken already and it had been easy, cathartic.

Ariel had never been easy for him.

But atonement required sacrifice.

And she was that.

"No. I'm here to ensure that the contract is honored. My brother has been freed, and he needs a wife."

"I don't suppose there's any chance of you trying to find another one."

"No. There is not. You were promised to my family, and my family has lost too much of what it is owed. I will not see this ended as well."

She tossed her hair, looking every bit the haughty American socialite he had always thought lurked beneath the rather sweet, large eyed demeanor that she had always portrayed when she came to visit Nazul. But it was not genuine. He could see that just as easily. She was trying to be brave.

"It seems a bit like crying over spilled milk," she said.

He was not a cruel man. But he was not a man who knew how to bend either. And there were certain things he refused to suffer. Fools, attempts at manipulation, and attitude from the woman whose father had engineered the murder of his parents.

"It is not milk that has been spilled, *ya amar*, but blood. The blood of my parents. And it is not spilled milk that causes anguish even now, but lost years. Fifteen years Riyaz has been in the dungeon. Fifteen years. Without human contact. With nothing. While I made the weapons that would claim his freedom. And you wish to speak to me in cliché. Let me return one for you. An eye for an eye. A tooth for a tooth. A life in captivity... For a life in captivity."

What she wanted didn't matter here. It could not matter. Softness here, with her, was unforgivable. A mistake made once before and never again.

Never again.

And then he reached out and took her by the arm, propelling her from her apartment. But she did not move quickly enough, so he lifted her off the ground with ease, cradling her in his arms as if she were a bride he were to carry over his own threshold. Laughable. She was not for him. She never had been. Always, from the beginning, she had been meant for Riyaz. And Riyaz had been robbed of... Absolutely everything.

It was that which fueled him now. The rage

that he felt on behalf of his brother. And the need to atone for his part in it.

He was dimly aware that she was punching him. But her fists were like pebbles against an oak. Of no consequence. His family had suffered. His only punishment had been to see it, when he'd deserved the same death.

All these years, he had lived a life. A life that was fueled by his need for revenge. A life that was purgatory, but a life all the same.

And she… She had been here in Paris. She had been everywhere. Living unfettered by the horror that had taken place at the palace. He did not pause to wait for the elevator, rather he carried her straight down the stairs of the old building, down and out to the street where his limousine was idling against the curb.

He opened the door on his own, and all but threw her onto the plush seat. He closed the door firmly and locked them in. "Drive," he said to his driver.

The man was paid well enough not to question anything. Which was good, because Ariel began to protest. And did not stop.

"He's kidnapping me," she said to the driver.

The driver's ice-cold glance connected with Cairo's in the rearview mirror. And then

Cairo slowly put the divider up between the front and the back of the car.

"He does not care," said Cairo.

"Cairo, what good does it do to have me marry your brother?" She looked around wildly, as if something suddenly dawned on her. "You don't really want me to marry him, do you? Am I going to be publicly executed or something? Since my father is already dead?"

"I told you already, it is not revenge I'm after," he said. "Public execution is barbaric. Your father was barbaric, Ariel. And if he were alive, perhaps I would treat him as he treated my family. It is a travesty that he was able to die so neatly. A heart attack. Bland, nondescript and far too quick. My mother screamed in agony. My father fought until his very last breath." She had the decency to look cowed by that. "It is not so simple as having you pay for his sins. It is about the restoration of Nazul. You were part of an original promise that was made to my country, to my brother. Your father was part of fracturing the peace of our country, the rightness of the world. What better image to present to the people than to see Riyaz back on the throne, with you as his bride, as if none of the bad things had ever happened?" He nearly laughed. For there was no erasing the past, no matter how beautifully you tried to gild the present. "Most importantly of all, it is what Riyaz has asked for." Though he wasn't sure his brother saw it how he did. But he had a plan in place to protect Ariel and please Riyaz. "The responsibility of restoring Nazul is mine."

"How is it yours?"

"Riyaz has been in a dungeon for fifteen years, how do you suppose he is?"

For the first time she looked subdued. "How is he?"

"Not well," he said. "When it becomes public knowledge that he lives…"

"It is," she said.

"I do not believe that it is."

"My mother knew. She texted me and she told me to run. Because Riyaz was out."

He paused for a long moment. "There must be somebody inside the palace with a connection to your family."

"Unlikely."

"We brought back many of the old staff who once worked there. Perhaps it was a mistake."

He was hell-bent on making things as they were. It was the only way. But in this… He had clearly miscalculated. Thankfully, however, it had not been leaked to the media at large. But who knew what Ariel's mother might do with it. She had never seemed like a craven or greedy woman, but then, neither had her husband. And he had been secretly plotting to aid in the overthrow of their family.

Yes, Cairo had learned at a very early age that you could not trust anyone.

"Regardless," he said. "We are attempting to ensure that Riyaz is ready. To face the public. There is a team with him now, and they are working with him."

"Are we going to the palace now?"

He was silent for a moment. "No. We must be certain that he is… For all that you might think that I am barbaric, that I would oversee your public execution, it is actually not my goal. So until I have made certain it is not my brother's, I will be keeping you safe. With me."

"With *you*?" She spoke the word as if it were laughable.

"Yes. I take my position in the monarchy very seriously. Riyaz is the heir, and I am the spare. But I was also the one who was spared captivity. It is my job now to use what I have to support him."

"And what is that?"

"Social graces," Cairo returned.

"I don't know that they've been on the best display."

"My apologies for your struggle," he said. "Cairo…"

"You knew. You knew I would come for you. You were prepared to run. Your mother was prepared to text you to run. Do not act surprised by it now."

"I had rather thought that murder would be the aim."

"No. So you should be relieved."

"I'm not."

He looked at her, hard. "This was always how it would be. You knew that. You knew it when you were a child. You know it now. The al Hadid family is an inevitability. We are the sun in the desert. You cannot outrun us. And you cannot extinguish us. Your fate is sealed."

CHAPTER TWO

THE SUN WAS so hot today. She felt like she might die of it, but she waited in the garden anyway. She waited and waited because she knew eventually...he would come.

"There you are, ya amar."

She looked up, the throb of her heart painful. "Cairo."

He'd told her she could call him by his name, and it had felt like a gift.

"Ari..."

The nickname on his lips made her feel a new kind of warm.

"Why doesn't Riyaz ever come out?"

"He's the heir. He's going to be the sheikh. Do you prefer his company to mine?"

She bit her lip. "I should."

His boyish grin became wicked. "But you don't."

If you could expire from panic, or perhaps have all the energy zapped out of you because you were in a state of heightened terror, then Ariel felt as if she had achieved that state. She had given up trying to talk to him. That snatch of memory was a lie. A joke.

That Cairo was long gone.

In many ways, he was dead, like she'd always imagined he was.

Because this wasn't her friend. This wasn't the boy she'd loved.

Her heart clenched tight.

Her father was responsible for this.

When she'd been a child, she'd been protected from the world. She'd had tutors at home, and she'd been well educated. She'd traveled all over. She'd been wealthy and comfortable. But she hadn't realized that the choices her father had made for her weren't… normal. Not in modern society.

She had been upset that she'd been promised to marry a sheikh, but her father had explained that people like them often had to make choices, alliances and marriages that others didn't. It was how you protected wealth, it was how you stayed safe, that was what he'd told her.

She'd accepted it then.

She couldn't say she was accepting of this now.

But there was some part of her that felt compelled to face this.

To see it through.

Even to the point of just…understanding what had become of Cairo over the course of all these years.

Or she could jump out of a moving vehicle and try to run for it.

They clearly weren't going to a major airport. They had passed Charles de Gaulle an hour ago, and she had no idea where they were headed. She also knew she didn't really have a hope in hell of getting away from him. She didn't have a phone. She could not be tracked. She had her backpack, which did have money in it, and if she could escape…

But then she would have to run, and he would only catch her. She should've been training to physically run, but she had been so certain that she would have time if this ever happened…

You were hoping it would never happen.

Yes. And it was a complicated hope. Of course it was. Because she had never wished lifelong captivity on Cairo. But of course, she had not wished to be caught up in their world again.

The whole of that world? Or just the version of it where you were promised to the wrong brother?

She shoved that thought aside and closed her eyes.

Cairo was alive.

He wasn't dead.

And so there she was, slumped in the corner of the limousine, and when they finally pulled in to the empty airfield, she was still trying to find…something to hold on to. She'd thought the longer she sat with him, with this, the more real it would seem.

But no.

It all felt less and less possible as the minutes ticked by.

And then she saw it. Shiny and sleek, cutting quickly through the air before descending smoothly, the sound it made following behind it.

"My private jet," he said.

"Right," she responded. "Naturally. Of course you have a private jet."

And she looked at him and realized. She had seen him. She had seen him in the media before. In society pages. But not under the name Cairo.

He was not the sort of playboy who posed for photos. There were often distant shots of him on yachts with half-naked beauties, sunglasses obscuring his face. She had not recognized him in those photos, though she'd be lying if she said she'd never stopped and given them a second look.

How could she not have realized it was Cairo? She'd looked twice at stories about Syed, because Cairo was the only man who'd ever made her look twice.

"Where did the name Syed come from?" she asked.

"One of my many names," he said, a grin curving his lips. "For a royal is gifted with many. And easy enough to adopt so that I could fly under the radar."

"You're a billionaire." She said it like an accusation.

"Yes," he said. "Staging a reverse coup isn't cheap."

"*How?* People don't just...become billion-aires."

"I had advantages. I had already taken on board the finest education the world had to offer, from the palace, of course. And then... I knew the right things to say. Knew some people to go to who could help me. Help me become somebody new. Help me navigate the system in England.

"I had nothing. Nothing but who and what I knew when I escaped. And now I have much. Much that I will pass on to my brother and to my people."

"So the plane doesn't belong to the royal family. It's yours."

"Yes, it is."

She felt overwhelmed then. Swamped by just how unmatched she was.

He was international businessman Syed al Shahar, and he was one of the most famous and highly sought-after men in the world. He had allies in every corner, and more than that, resources. And they would be going back to a country where he was a prince. A sheikh. And there... Well, there she would have no allies at all.

She was an ant compared to him.

Her father had been nothing but a trifling fool who'd had no idea what he was messing with.

And he had condemned her and her mother to a life of worry.

He had condemned Cairo's family to death.

No. She would never forgive him. And hadn't.

He had made so much money betraying them. Her mother had taken much of it in court. And they had never spoken to him again. He had died alone. So for all that Cairo knew of her father's demise, she was not certain that he was aware of that.

She didn't feel like telling him now. Because it felt a small part of her power. If he did not know everything about her. Unless…

"You've always known where I was, haven't you?"

"Yes."

"Why did you only come and get me now?"

It sounded small, and a bit like a plea, and she hated herself for it.

"I felt it reasonable to allow you to have a life while there was a life for you to have. One of your choosing. But there are things bigger than you at play here. Bigger than me. Choice is not for us. You have done quite well for yourself in the fashion industry."

"Thank you for noticing," she said.

The fashion industry was cutthroat, especially in Paris. And she knew that her position in it was enhanced by her father's position in society, made extra grim by the fact that she was no longer speaking to him when he died. And yet it was still his name that she often traded on.

But she had ambition, and it was the way the world worked.

"I particularly like your jewelry."

"Thank you," she said. "Although I can't tell if you're being serious or not."

"I am. I have an appreciation of art," he said. "Why would I lie?"

"Only because I did not think that you would be concerned with such things."

"Many of my mistresses have enjoyed your pieces."

She looked at him. His dark eyes were filled with fire she could not divine.

And she didn't know why, but the statement about *mistresses* made her stomach feel hollow. It was something of a reminder of the gulf between them. But then, there had always been a gulf between them. She could remember when they were young, there had always been something shining in his eyes, a knowledge and mischief that she could not quite get a grasp on.

But then, Cairo had never been hers to grasp. They had a strange friendship back at the palace, but it had never been easy. It had always felt as if there was a wall between them, by some necessity.

"It is nice that you are such a conscientious paramour," she said. Rather than any of the other things that had crowded her throat.

"Let's go," he said, opening the door of the limousine, but she remained resolutely stuck to the spot.

"Are you really going to make it this difficult?"

"Should I make it easy?"

Tension stretched between them, and he reached across the space and pulled her to him.

His body was hard, hot. And suddenly, she wanted to lean into it. Into his strength. Into the way that he held her closely.

It was the strangest thing.

This urge to surrender.

So she struggled. Against herself more than anything, but he did not seem bothered by it. Not at all. He extracted her from the limousine and carried her to the doors of the private plane.

And he hauled her right up the steps.

She kicked and struggled, and there was a smiling flight attendant on board. She looked at the other woman in disbelief. The other woman simply smiled. "Can I get you some champagne?"

"Are you..." she asked. "This man is *kidnapping* me."

She only grinned wider. Like a terrifying fem-bot. "Sheikh Cairo is of course the ruler of that which he surveys, and the reigning power in this facility. I assure you that it is functionally impossible for him to kidnap anyone in this sphere."

"I assure you it's not," she said, still wiggling as he set her down on one of the seats inside the cabin.

"Champagne?" the woman asked again.

"You're all shocking," she said. *"Complicit,"* she added for good measure.

"No champagne then?"

"Of course I want champagne," Ariel snapped.

And she let the grinning woman pour her a glass of champagne, and she felt slightly like she'd lost some sort of battle, but she was on the plane with or without a drink, so she might as well indulge.

She took the glass from the woman, who smiled and turned to Cairo. "None for me. You may go."

He didn't use her name or accept her services and Ariel felt slightly irritated that she'd accepted.

And the woman vanished. Just as he'd commanded.

"Do you have her under a spell?"

"Yes, Ariel. That spell is called power." He reclined in his chair, his hands behind his head, tightening his shirt over his broad, muscular chest.

She was trying to wrap her head around the fact that this was both Syed and Cairo. When she'd seen him at her house he'd been recognizable only as Cairo. It was the impact of him, his eyes, and the fact he'd appeared right after her mother's text.

But now, with him on the private jet, sprawled out like a man waiting to be served, she saw the infamous playboy and businessman. She was shocked they'd never moved in the same circles; in fashion she interacted with many men like him, and as he'd said, he bought her jewelry for his mistresses.

But it was by design. She knew that. She didn't even have to ask.

"You've changed," she said.

"I would hope so," he responded, his tone dark. "My parents were murdered and I was separated from my brother and my homeland. I ought to have changed."

For the first time, regret and pity swamped the rest of what she felt. Overtook her concerns for herself.

"I'm sorry. For what you went through, I really am. I felt like I lost something that day too."

His eyes went hard, and she knew she'd miscalculated. "You were never happy there."

"I wasn't happy I was being forced into marriage. Show me a girl who would be?"

"My brother is the ruler of Nazul. Many women would line up for the chance."

"I never wanted to be a wife. By which I

mean I never wanted to be defined by that. My mother's whole identity was my father. She just…went along with everything he said. She loved me, she loves me. But she…she doesn't know how to make up her own mind. She doesn't take a stand, ever. She's never known how to be alone or single. It's why we don't see each other very much now. She's had two husbands since my dad." She shook her head. "Why would I want that? Maybe I wouldn't have wanted to get married at all. Maybe I don't like men. No one ever asked me."

His lips curved upward, his head tilting to the side. "Do you not?"

"Do I not what?"

"Like men."

She'd wondered about it, in her years since leaving Nazul. There hadn't been a single man who'd turned her head in all the years since Cairo had offered her an orange. She'd been a girl then, and it was distant enough memory that she sometimes wondered if she'd imagined it.

"I like my work," she said. "I like choosing. I like being free. I like cashmere sweatpants and evenings at home alone. I like ice cream and costume dramas and I really do not think I will make a good wife or a good sheikha."

"You didn't answer my question."

"I gave you all the information you need."

She could tell he wasn't used to people talking to him like that. His jaw went stiff, his hands tightening on the arms of the chair he sat in. Fine. He had already kidnapped her. He had already taken her memories, her best and sweetest memories, of Nazul and turned them into something else.

She'd wept for him.

She'd loved him.

The boy.

Not the man he was now.

"Why do you need to know? You don't care what I like. You don't care what I want."

"A good point."

"Would my lack of interest in men keep you from marrying me off to your brother?"

"No. This is not about you. It's about what Riyaz has asked for. What he feels is best for Nazul. You do not matter at all, apart from that which you symbolize."

And like that, all the pity for him evaporated. "How dare you? How dare you speak to me like that, as if you can simply…"

"Oh, forgive me, Ariel, do you find it confronting that you have to live a life you didn't choose? I'm not your audience."

"Such a caustic tone is a bit basic, don't you think?"

He arched a dark brow. "I am anything but basic, *ya amar*. And I think you know that."

Ariel knew how to pretend to be fine. She knew how to pretend to be bored even when she was nervous. She had learned how to navigate the often harsh fashion industry, and that had been easy compared to recovering from what her father had done. To living with the knowledge that her freedom might have an expiration date on it. And well, Cairo was right about one thing. That information was not new. Not in the least. She had known that she would be married off to somebody from the time that she was a child. Then her father had committed that horrible act and she'd been worried the retribution would fall on her head. It was only in the small window of her life that she had allowed herself to imagine that her fate might not be fixed.

So yes. She knew how to pretend to be bored. She knew how to banter with people who actively wished her ill. She did not allow herself to be affected overly much by the opinions of others. Because she alone knew her own strength. She had to.

She would love to say that she had been close with her mother in the years since her father's death. She'd wondered at the time if she might change when the structure of the family changed. But it was like the whole thing hadn't been a release, more that it had dissolved everything.

His betrayal. His death.

They had never been able to be whole again after all of that.

And it was as if it was easier for her mother to go off and have her own life. They spoke on the phone. They texted. But Helene seemed much happier with distance between them, and Ariel didn't see the point in fighting that. There were too many things to fight. And she had chosen in these years to focus on herself and her goals. Because…

Well. Because of things like this.

He was watching her. Far too closely.

"Do you think that you might be able to read my mind? And even if you could, would it matter?"

"One should always attempt to know as much is possible about the person they find themselves thirty thousand feet in the air with, don't you think?"

"I don't know what I think. In fact, I think I won't know what I think for the duration. I would rather give you nothing." And that was true. She wanted to hide all of her feelings.

Her fears. Her desires. The strange, tangled up grief that she had felt for him for all these years.

She wanted to hide it all.

If he wanted a vessel, a symbol, then she could be that. And give him nothing of what she was.

And what will the point of your life be then?

She wished that she had an answer to that. She suddenly felt sad. Bleak. Because what had the point of any of it been? She had built her life up to a certain place, and now would have to abandon it. So what had been the point of building it up at all? Giving herself a taste of a life that she could not hold on to. A taste of the life that she could not claim or keep.

And apparently Riyaz wasn't in his right mind.

"You're afraid," he said.

"You say that as if it's a flaw?"

"Not at all. Simply an observation. I told you. I'm not going to hurt you."

"You seem to think that the only way a person can be hurt is with a sword. I had a life."

"So did I. And I abandoned it."

"Have you sold all of your holdings? Are you releasing hold on everything that you've built?"

"Of course not. It is advantageous to my country to keep it. But it will not be my primary focus. My days of traveling around the world and doing as I please are at an end. I was always working to accomplish the goal of taking back Nazul, but I knew I would have to get back to my other life. The life from before. Which was also disrupted. We are not guaranteed the life that we plan, are we? You will forgive me for not feeling sympathy where perhaps you think I should. It is this… This generation. This modern world. You think that you can simply pursue your own selfish version of happiness, and that you are guaranteed such a thing, entitled to it. But we are entitled to nothing. I am royalty and I learned that. I learned that as I watched my parents died. As my brother was taken away from me. As I had to run, knowing that it was the right thing to do even though it felt like cowardice. I wanted to stay and fight to the death as my father did. That was what I wanted. Hero's death. But I had to find a way to make a hero's life, did I not? Because of Riyaz. And so… That is what I'm doing."

"A hero's life," she said softly. And she knew that she would be revealing herself with her next words, so she chose them carefully. "And yet, for all that I have heard of you in the guise of Syed, you have chosen a play-boy's life. And as you admitted to me, you've had many mistresses. How does that match up with what you're telling me? How does that equate to heroism? How do you look at yourself and see what you claim?"

"I did not say that I looked at myself and saw a hero. I am in pursuit of it. There is an inequality that I must balance. I had fifteen years of freedom while my brother was in chains. I had fifteen more years of life as my parents have laid in the graves. I can never wholly right this." His eyes went blank. "But as of now, I live in service, in an attempt to make amends of some kind."

"Where are we going?"

"I have a home in the mountains near my country. It was a way that I could sneak in with the enemy unaware. A compound that my brother does not know exists."

"I'm confused. Are you doing things in *service* of your brother, or are you *afraid* of your brother?"

"I do not fear him. But I also do not know his frame of mind. I do not know how deeply his time in the dungeon damaged him. That, I await, before I go crashing in to his world."

She looked at him, and then she saw the boy that he had been. The boy who had come and sat with her at the fountain. The boy who'd cared. He was worried about his brother. And she should not feel any sympathy for him. None at all. She should not feel… He had kidnapped her. What was the matter with her? Why was she finding ways to justify his behavior? To excuse him?

Was it because he was handsome?

No, it was because he was handsome that she wanted to fling herself out of the plane. Because for all these years no man had turned her head. For all these years she had told herself that the tied up, twisted up feelings that Cairo had once made her feel were locked away in the past. And yet, he was here. And she was tied up. Twisted up.

There was a syndrome for feeling sympathy for one's captor. She was a modern enough woman to be aware of it.

Except he has been something more to you. And you can't un-know that.

And your father did *destroy his family.*

Her father had claimed that he had not known that the men who were there to take over the country would kill the royal family. He had claimed that. But even at fourteen, she had not found herself to be that naive. She knew better. Her father could not possibly have believed that his betrayal would not have resulted in the deaths of the family. He had to know. And yet...

She wondered if he told himself that. She wondered if he told himself that there was nothing he could've done. That he had believed in good faith and done what he needed to do to keep his family safe. It was the narrative that he had told them. That he had been put in an impossible position where they were threatened.

It was only that... She had not believed it. Neither had her mother. What they had believed was that he had wanted that money, and it superseded the influence of the royal family, after all, the royal family would cease to have influence if they were deposed... And that was the issue. It seemed very much like he had known what would happen. And perhaps he had felt that it would happen no matter what, and there would be no gain for him at all if he didn't help.

But there was no honor in it. And she could never respect it.

And that created a strange sort of responsibility inside of her for Cairo's feelings. No matter that she had shouted at him that it wasn't her sin, it was her father's. Perhaps in the same way that he felt responsible for his bloodline, for Riyaz, she felt responsible for her father.

Not responsible enough to marry Riyaz. But…

"How much longer?"

"So impatient. You must remember my country is beautiful."

"I barely remember it at all," she lied.

"You were to be the queen. Did you not find that an intoxicating idea of the future?"

She shook her head. "No. I never wanted power. And when you are being moved about by powerful men, I do not think that the promise of the throne feels powerful at all." She looked at a spot, just behind his head because looking at him was always a mistake. "I was always being maneuvered. And I was very aware of it. I never thought that there was power to be had for me."

"And if there was?"

She met his gaze again. "What do you mean?"

"It remains to be seen, how Riyaz will do."

"So what, you think that I might need to…"

"I don't know. But you are successful. You are more than a socialite now. And that… I think that that is a boon. There is an appearance of modernity to you as a choice, and the country is in bad need of some. It's been cut off from the outside world for fifteen years after being nearly crushed beneath the bootheel of a dictator."

"Oh. Well. I didn't know that you are aiming to bring the country into the modern era. The whole forced bride thing seems to belie that."

"*Appearances*, I said."

"Yes. You are all about those, aren't you?"

"Life is all about appearances, Ariel. I appeared to be a simple orphan boy, and managed to construct a new identity for myself as a result. I appeared to be an international playboy without an original thought in my head, and therefore was able to get close to the enemies of my family. I appeared harmless. Therefore I was able to inflict great harm when necessary. Appearance is all life is."

"I don't believe that."

There was a core of steel running through his words. It made her tremble. It frightened her.

He was not the man that he once had been. But then, she had known him as a boy. He also wasn't the playboy that he appeared to be, she did believe that. She believed him capable of great ruthlessness. And she did not ever want to fall on the wrong side of that. But at the same time… There was something about him, about the way that he was. The way that he was put together. It made her tremble.

It called to something long forgotten inside of her.

Whispered across her skin like an orange scented breeze.

She shut her mind down. She was panicking, that's what she was doing. She was seeking desperately for something... Something other than panic. And that was twisting it all into this... Whatever it was. She refused to name it.

Refused.

"There is a bedroom at the back. Why don't you sleep? For when we land, we will be assessing the situation. And you will begin training."

"I'm not a dog," she said. "'Go lie down.' 'Begin your training.'"

He said nothing. And so she sat, sipping her champagne slowly and staring straight ahead. And even when she became utterly exhausted, she refused to sleep.

Because she would not give him the satisfaction of having successfully given her a command.

CHAPTER THREE

WHEN THE PLANE descended over the mountains, in a strip of land that fell between countries, onto the hidden airway concealed by a pass, he felt like the blood of his ancestors had risen up within him. The battle cry of a warrior echoing through his body.

It had nothing to do with Ariel being at his side.

He was home. And he had returned home a victor. As he had known he must. Ariel was still sitting across from him, staring, though he wondered if she had lapsed off into some fugue state. She certainly didn't want to give him the satisfaction of being reasonable. Pity for her, he was neither satisfied nor dissatisfied by her display of temper. He had bigger things on his mind. And indeed, there were bigger problems set out before himself and his nation.

Ariel was meant to be a solution.

Atonement.

She did not possess the power to become a problem.

Riyaz had demanded her. Cairo would fulfill the promise.

After the plane landed, the door opened, and she remained. Sitting. Looking straight ahead.

"If you have the idea that I will not take you in hand and bodily remove you, I believe I have already disproven such a notion."

"Why must you make everything about you?"

She stood and disembarked on the plane on her own two feet, and he could only stare.

He remembered her well from his time at the palace, though he had spent many years attempting to not remember at all.

He tried not to remember that life. For it created an ache in his chest that had no home. It could not.

He could not allow such a thing to take up residence within him. No. Not when he himself was far too essential to this cause.

There could not be a moment of self-pity. And so, he did not cast his mind back. But she… She forced him to think of those days.

He thought of his brother, as he had once

been. His older brother, his idol in every way. Much more serious than he had ever been.

And the only sticking point ever in their relationship was one that Riyaz had not known about.

His eyes drifted to Ariel.

What a foolish boy he'd been.

He had loved it when the sulky American girl had come to stay with them. She was beautiful.

She had been quite the most singular thing he'd ever seen with her aqua blue eyes and pale blond hair. Her lips were the most delicate shade of pink, and his thoughts of Ariel had been his very first thoughts that were quite so... Specific. He had thought of kissing those lips.

Devouring them.

As a teenage boy, it had made him ache. She had made him ache. And she had been for his brother. And so, all he had been able to do was... He remembered stolen moments in the garden, and he was certain they had not been quite the same for him.

And now?

She was no less beautiful. She was singular.

Of course he had kept tabs on her. But the

photographs of her in the media did not do her justice.

And he marveled at his own behavior. Buying her jewelry for his cast-off lovers. In many ways, he wondered if it was an intentional nod to that first experience of desire.

Of course, she was twenty-eight years old now. Likely the innocence of youth had long been banished for her, as it certainly had for him.

She is no concern of yours. Not beyond bringing her here.

As a green boy, he'd let himself get far too close to temptation.

He'd been playing with fire. But he knew better now.

She was here for Riyaz. Nothing more. She had always been for Riyaz.

It was only a twenty-minute ride by helicopter from this home down to the palace in the capital city. They were close. And yet, Riyaz did not know of their presence.

Necessary.

He needed to speak to Brianna. And he would. Soon.

"Come," he said.

"Where?" She looked around them. And he knew what she saw. Forbidding, harsh wilderness, which seemed to have nothing hospitable to it at all.

"It is an oasis. In the desert."

"You are delusional," she said. "I have a feeling you would call a thimbleful of water an oasis in the desert if you thought you could use such assertions to manipulate those around you."

"Perhaps I might," he said. "But in this case, it is not a thimbleful. Follow me."

There was a thin trail that wound its way through the mountain passage. They were arid mountains, with twisted olive trees covering the rocky surfaces. Scrub brush down beneath. The sky was an insipid sort of blue, washed pale by the heat of the Arabian sunshine.

"Are there snakes?" she asked.

"I would have thought you'd know. There are snakes everywhere. One must always look out."

She looked at him, those turquoise eyes regarding him closely. And he could see that she was not certain whether he'd spoken in metaphor or not. "Literal and figurative," he clarified.

"Of course."

He led the way, but paused for a moment. "The plane is already gone. If you attempt to run… There is but one place you can go. And it contains me. Think on that."

"I'm not stupid enough to run away from you in the desert."

"That is a relief."

"If I was going to attempt a reckless run-away situation, I would have leapt out of the car."

"That begs the question… Why didn't you?"

"If I had managed to survive the fall without injuring myself, I would not have been able to outrun you. What is the point of suffering the humiliation of such a thing if I can't even really escape?"

"A valid question."

"I wish that I could ask you what happened. How we ended up here. But the sad thing is I know the answer. And so… I'm just following you."

"The best decision, you will find."

They came around the corner of one of the black craggy outcroppings, and there you could see, glinting in the sun, a sheet of glass. The front of the house.

"What is this?"

"My fortress."

It was a stark, black box. All tinted windows in the front that kept out the harshness of the desert sun, but provided a brilliant view of their surroundings. It was part of the wild landscape. And it was also a shelter.

"You can only get in if your palm print is programmed to allow you to do so." They walked up to a mighty gate that cordoned off the property from the surrounding land. He pressed his palm against a flat black box at the gate, and it gave them entry.

"Are there any vehicles here?"

"Yes," he said. "But like the gate, you will not be using them unless you have custom access."

"One might be tempted to call you paranoid," she said.

"One would be tempted to respond that my paranoia is earned. Do you not think?"

She said nothing. And he was gratified by the fact he had won this round. Or perhaps she really was getting tired now.

As they approached the home, its massive structure shaded them, and he walked up to the door and placed his palm against the sensor he knew was there. It unlocked.

It was all black inside, flooded with light. "This is…"

"It's extraordinary," he said. "I am aware. I have been working on it for many years. A place for me to set up operations as I worked to amass a team to take out the corrupt leadership of my nation, and free my brother."

"How did you… How did you do that? You're one man. You're not an army."

"That is correct. I am only one man. But I am Sheikh Cairo, and the protection of my country is my sworn duty. My loyalty to my brother is unparalleled. Do you know what the function of the second son is in a traditional royal family?"

"You were to join the military. To become the commander."

"Yes. Did we have that conversation once?"

She shook her head slowly. "We didn't. I asked Riyaz once, when he went walking with me out at the fountain."

"Did my brother walk with you?"

She looked at him. "Yes."

He had not known that. The sensation that assaulted his chest was a shock to him. Why should he feel… Anything over the fact that his brother had taken walks with the woman that had been promised to be his wife? It was good and right that Riyaz should do so.

It was only that he had assumed the two of them did not have a connection then. He had thought… He had thought the connection was his. And his alone.

It mattered not. She was not his. Not then. Not now.

Part of him wanted to take her back to Paris then. She would not be within his reach, but she would not be within reach of Riyaz either.

The deep desire to do just that shook him down to his core.

He would not. He would not falter, not now. He couldn't trust himself. Could not trust himself especially when it came to her.

He could see she did not want this, but...to give in to her needs would be to deny Riyaz.

And it would be to indulge himself.

That weighted the scale. It meant he had to persevere in this. To give Riyaz what he wanted.

To deny Ariel in this was also to deny himself. And if he'd learned one thing from his failure fifteen years ago...

It was that he had to deny himself at all costs.

"Aisha," he called out.

A small woman wearing traditional robes appeared. "Please show Ariel to her room. Have a bath drawn for her. She and I are to dine together tonight. Where we will speak of future plans."

"I did not agree to have dinner with you," she said.

Something like a flame ignited in his gut.

"I think you still do not understand the situation in which you find yourself, Ariel Hart.

"You do not have a choice here. You are in this territory between countries. Traditionally, it is no man's land. But now? It is my land. And in it you will do as I say. In it, I am lord and master. You will go, you will bathe. You will perfume your skin, you will put on jewels and that gown that is befitting of a royal woman in this country, and we will speak of the future."

A challenge glittered in her eyes, and he knew that whether he wanted to or not, he was going to have to see where the challenge led. For he could not ensure that she would do as he asked unless he put her in the bathtub himself and scrubbed his hands over her skin.

The idea sent a jolt of unexpected lust through him.

Lust was something he felt on his own timetable. He had spent a great many years exorcising demons in bed. He had found that anonymous sex did a lot to banish unpleasant memories. But there were times when he indulged and times when he did not. He had spent years availing himself to every perversion known to man. The sheer variety of it all had turned him rather jaded. And it was best to be jaded, he found. For that allowed him dominion over his sexual desire. So having it rise up now with little warning or control was… It was unacceptable.

He gritted his teeth and tamped it down. His boyhood desire for Ariel had been that of an untried lad. He had not known what it was like to sink into a woman's body, and so she had consumed his thoughts. He knew now. From every angle and every position. There was no mystery left. And yet, Ariel felt like a mystery.

She belongs to Riyaz.

Yes. She belongs to Riyaz.

He snapped his fingers, and Aisha put her hand on Ariel's arm.

"Come along," she said.

"I will," said Ariel. And then she turned aqua eyes on to him. "But only to get away from him."

As if that would affect him. He felt nothing. The sooner she understood that, the better.

CHAPTER FOUR

SHE WAS TRYING not to be impressed by the grandeur of this place. At first she had thought it terribly ugly. A large, shiny box out in the middle of these unforgiving mountains.

But she could see the beauty once she was inside. The way the windows captured the sunlight, while protecting them from the harshest aspects of it. The way it showed them the mountains, the trees, the wild landscape below, while concealing the house from view.

It was an architectural wonder.

A huge part of fashion was appreciating the elements of design, and this house was... It was truly remarkable.

The woman was at least a head taller than Ariel, but she moved with a ruthless efficiency that belied her size. She opened up a door in the hallway, black like everything else, and Ariel's mouth opened when she saw the room. It too was black. The floors, the walls. But the ceiling had a graphic, brilliant wallpaper on it with large magenta flowers. A chandelier hung from the ceiling. The bed that stood at the center of the room was gold, with plush, velvet coverings in different shades of pink.

"What is this room for?"

"It has always been for you," she said. "Sheikh Cairo has been preparing this place for this inevitability for many years."

The words echoed within her.

Riyaz had demanded her. But Cairo had prepared a room for her.

As if it had been fate.

No.

He had never been her fate. That was all magical thinking, the kind she'd let herself fall into as a girl.

She wasn't a girl anymore.

"Has he?" The words came out scratchy.

"Yes. I will just go run your bath. The bathroom is just through there. You will find a selection of clothing in the armoire. You may choose that which you wish for dinner." The woman disappeared, and a moment later she heard water running.

She opened up the gilded, mirrored armoire, and inside found a myriad of jeweled, ornate dresses.

They were halfway between contemporary and traditional dress, each one of vibrant color, with gems stitched into fashionable designs.

The designer's heart within her quickened. This was inspiration. Down to the depths of her soul.

And she felt... Privileged to get to put on such clothing. But she didn't want to give him the satisfaction of knowing that.

She might be enjoying elements of this, but he didn't need the satisfaction of knowing that.

She touched a brilliant blue gown. It had a matching top that would bare her midriff, and a skirt with a high waist that looked as if it would hug her hips and flare out around her knees.

She selected it and carried it into the bathroom. And what she saw in there stopped her cold. It was not a simple bathtub. Rather more of a pool, with gold taps, the farthest most edge simply a window that looked out at the desert below.

"I will leave you," the woman said. "The water is scented with oil, and you will find different scrubs at the edge just there."

"Thank you," Ariel said.

It was funny how, even now, her manners

seemed important. What a strange thing that was. Though none of the staff here had been rude to her. Other than the whole…not caring that she'd been kidnapped thing.

It made her feel compelled to be polite.

The woman left, and she began to undress slowly, shivering as she realized she stood naked there in front of the windows, gazing out at the wilderness. There was no one and nothing there, of course.

The sun spilled into the room and illuminated her naked body, gold poured out on her curves. It warmed her.

And it felt to her a rather wanton thing. And she had never played the part of a wanton in her entire life.

It was thrilling. Standing there looking out with her body exposed, and she could not say why. But it was like she was on the precipice of flying. On the edge of freedom.

You are not free. You're a captive.

That sobering thought cut off the strange fantasy she'd found herself caught in, and she began to walk into the water.

She moaned as the warmth enveloped her body. She really was exhausted. The bath was deep, and huge, and she swam to the window. She was still entirely exposed. Even covered in water.

She thought of Cairo, his intense, hot gaze, and she felt her nipples go tight, her breasts get heavy.

Something began to throb between her legs.

And she was so tired she couldn't even shut the feelings away.

In her mind's eye, she saw him hand her the orange again. But this time, it was Cairo the man. And she was naked. In a pool of water.

His eyes were hot. Dark with hunger...

She had to wonder if she was here because he'd forced her, or if because part of her had waited fifteen years to be with Cairo again...

She gasped, snapped herself back to reality and went over to the scrubbing salts.

She put some on her hand and began to work them vigorously over her body, abrading herself, punishing herself for such thoughts.

She shivered. Then she rinsed herself and got out of the water. She dried herself on the plushiest towel that had ever made contact with her skin, and put on the heavy, jeweled garment she had chosen for herself.

A moment later, there was a knock at the door. "I am here for hair and makeup," said a woman that she had not yet seen before.

"I'm sure that isn't necessary."

"You are having dinner with *him*." She said

the pronoun as if it were capitalized. Singular. "Of course it is necessary."

What was it about this man? All of these employees talked about him as if he was the sun and the moon.

And she decided she would ask the woman just that. She wasn't too polite to not be nosy. She sat down in a chair in front of the mirror.

"How many of you work here?"

"At least fifty are employed here. To keep house, to cook, to take care of the grounds. As security."

"And why are you so loyal to Cairo?"

"He saved us," the woman said, admiration overtaking her voice. "After the royal family was deposed, many politically connected families were in danger. And there were some of us who were impoverished before, and in danger of going hungry. He ran missions where he smuggled many of us over the border. And he ensured that we were well cared for afterward. Sheikh Cairo never forgot his people. And now, he is on the verge of bringing us home. On the verge of restoring that which the locusts have eaten. He is our savior."

"No wonder he has a god complex," she said. But a knot had begun to form in her chest, because she could not deny that what he had done was good.

And why was he treating her as he did?

"You are going to marry Riyaz," the woman said. "We pray for our sheikh."

"Yes," she said. "I will too."

She had to hope for…something to come from Riyaz. Compassion that Cairo certainly wasn't showing her. Something.

She hadn't had a choice about whether or not she came here. She didn't have a choice about whether or not she'd be sent to Riyaz. Cairo hadn't saved *her*. And if Riyaz wasn't sane…if he was bent on vengeance, well, she didn't know what that meant for her fate.

CHAPTER FIVE

"HE ISN'T WELL."

He looked at Brianna's worried golden eyes. "No improvement?"

"He does not sleep in a bed, Cairo. He outright refuses the meals that we serve. He works out, punishing his body day and night…"

"I have freed him," Cairo said. "I do not understand why he persists in acting this way."

"Because in his mind he is still in a cage, Cairo. And I do not know how to reach him."

"I have faith in you," he said.

Brianna's expression softened. He had often thought that perhaps if he were to marry a woman it might've been her. But he worried that she had been treated too harshly, and he wanted to protect her. Not expose her to more harm.

Brianna deserved a different sort of man. A man who could love.

His own had been killed one night out in the desert.

She deserved to be well rid of him and Riyaz as soon as she finished her work.

He knew that she admired him. He knew that he would've been able to seduce her easily. But he actually knew her. Cared for her. So he had never done so. She was more a sister to him. Though he knew the description would likely cause her distress.

"It's difficult," Brianna said. "I can't force him to talk about what he doesn't want to remember."

"Keep trying."

He heard footsteps and looked up over his phone screen. And there she was, standing in the doorway. Her presence was a punch of pure adrenaline that took his breath away. The blue that she was wearing made her eyes look like jewels lit on fire. And it was the strip of her revealed midriff that caused his body to stir. How long had it been since such a simple show of skin on a woman had created such a response in him? Perhaps never.

"Let me show you something."
Her eyes went round. "What?"

"A secret." She looked at him as if he were magic, and he felt like he'd won a prize, even though he knew that he was risking much by taking her hand this way and leading her down the cool palace corridor.

He pushed open the door to the room that held the wedding gems.

He didn't know why he wanted to show her these.

Perhaps because he found himself imagining giving them to her.

But they would never be his to give. Not to her or anyone.

"What are they?" she asked, approaching the glass case, her eyes alight with wonder as she looked at the jewels. Bracelets, a necklace, glittering ruby red. And the red silk scarf...

"Wedding jewels. For the sheikha and the sheikh."

Her eyes met his then, and he saw pain there.

"I have to go," he said, ending the call abruptly.

"Was that one of your lovers?" Ariel asked.

She said it casually. But she sounded jealous.

"Did you not hear what we were speaking of?"

Ariel shrugged. "I heard a woman's voice."

"I do not ever speak to my lovers on the phone. There is never a reason to. That was one of my oldest friends. She is overseeing Riyaz."

"And?"

"Progress is yet to be made. But I trust her."

"So you do trust some people," she said.

"I rescued her," he said. "She is bound to me. Who better to trust?"

"You have a habit of that," she said. "Rescuing people, I mean."

"What makes you say that?"

"The woman who did my hair and makeup. She told me. About how everyone in your employ was smuggled out of the country. That you saved them."

"Brianna is not from Nazul," he said. "But yes."

"Brianna," she said. "Is that the woman with Riyaz?"

"It is. She is a very dear friend."

"Forgive me," she said. "But you do not seem like the sort of person who has friends. Though I will concede that perhaps I only feel this way because of the way that we reconnected with one another."

"Glad I could surprise you," he said.

What he did not like, was the way his body was responding to her. It was very deep and elemental. And it was unacceptable. The way that he had once felt about Ariel was immaterial. And it should not be bleeding into this present moment. But she was... Stunning. No photograph or media had prepared him. He had any number of beautiful women. Of course he had. He was a man with money and influence. A man with power. It was an aphrodisiac, even without what he knew to be physical attributes that women enjoyed.

But there was something different about her. There always had been. He despised that. That there should be something singular about this woman.

It made no sense as to why. "Come," he said. He stood and held out his hand. Determined to touch her now, because he would defy this attraction between them. He would make it his own. Force it into submission. He was not controlled by his body.

It was one of the assets of years of hedonism.

For him, there was nothing yet to discover.

Except for her.

Women were all the same. He placed that thought firmly in his mind. She did not reach out to take his hand, so he took it on his own.

A sharp gasp exited her lips, and she looked up at him, her eyes wide.

"Come," he repeated. "We will go to dinner."

"All right," she said, tilting her chin upward. Her hand was soft. It was the bland list of observations. Women's hands were often soft, and Ariel did not do manual labor. Why would her hand be anything but soft?

And yet he had not expected her palm to feel as the silken petal of a desert lily. He had not anticipated that it would be something beyond mere softness, but a home that seemed to slip beneath the barrier of his soul and create in him a dry well of longing that was like a man who needed drink in the desert. The sensation that one might die if they could not satiate that need.

Oh, yes. He had expected that she would be soft. But he had not expected this.

Ruthlessly, he shut that down. And he led her from the seating area where he had been speaking to Brianna, into the dining room. The table was laid with a grand feast. Traditional meals of his country.

It was one of the many benefits he enjoyed for having rescued so many people from his homeland. There was a great deal of incredible traditional cooking in his life, and he did not take it for granted. For his people had been overrun. His people had been oppressed these many years.

Seeing where the spirit endured was part of what had given him motivation. Strength. Hope. For as much as he was dark, gritty and forged in the iron of pain, hope resided. It must.

One did not seek to seize back the throne without hope. Even now, the endeavor that they were undertaking with Riyaz required hope.

For Riyaz had suffered unimaginably. And Cairo had to cling to hope that they could bring his brother back from the brink. There was no other option.

Not for his country, and not for him.

Cairo was the only family Riyaz had left. Cairo and Ariel were the only remaining links to the past beyond the food on this table. Beyond traditions and remembered songs and stories. The whisper from the window that reminded him of his mother's voice.

Riyaz was all he had.

He looked up at Ariel. "I hope this is to your liking."

"I... I don't know why I feel the need to reassure you," she said.

"I don't know. Do I seem a man in need of great reassurance?"

"I just find it interesting that I am compelled to ensure that I'm not rude to my kidnapper."

"Perhaps because you know I am not your kidnapper. Rather, your trustee. Your guardian."

"Please." She sat down in the chair just to the right of the head of the table, and he took his place at the head.

"Is it to your liking?"

"Is my answer important? Yet again, I did not think that my preferences signified."

"Oh, they change nothing of note. But they may actually change the menu. So it would not be the worst thing in the world for you to voice your opinions on the cuisine."

"It looks lovely," she said. "Truly. And there, now I have successfully done something to ease the monster of rising Stockholm syndrome inside of me."

"Stockholm syndrome? Have you begun to sympathize with me?"

"Don't go that far."

"But would you like some jeweled couscous? Perhaps some lamb?"

"Yes."

He did the honors of dishing out the feast.

And he presented her a plate laden with delicacies, and he was gratified when he saw the rising hunger in her eyes. And he felt an answering hunger rising inside of him that had nothing to do with food. This woman had always fascinated him. She was something quite a bit beyond anything he'd ever experienced before. And always had been. Yet again he wondered if that had something to do with the fact that when he'd met her he had been nothing more than a virgin boy. A boy who knew nothing about desire. Whose first taste of it had been when sitting near her. Was it possible that it was simply such an experience that was so formative that one never truly moved beyond it?

Perhaps it was his punishment, for his sins.

Or perhaps it was just a reminder of his weakness.

"I do not wish to fight with you," he said. Because there was no point to that. She could fight him all she wanted, but his mission would not change. If she thought she might wear him down, she was incorrect. If she thought she might eventually appeal to some sort of sympathy inside of him, she was incorrect there as well. He did not possess any. He could not feel sorry for a woman who was bound to a life of finery and protection. He would see no harm done to her, and she would enjoy an elevated position. There were true hardships in the world. Having choice taken away from you was hardly one of them. Especially not when the cage you would be put in was so finely gilded.

Everyone had cages.

"Why do you wish to know anything about me?" she asked.

"Because. We are to be family. Should we not know one another?"

"Then you tell me first. How did you decide to start a chain of hotels that would make you a billionaire? How did you get into property management, and innovation? How did you know that it would make you the kind of successful that you needed to be in order to claim your country again?"

"I looked at the success of other men who had done similar things. Men who had come up from nothing. And I used the information that I had about what made men envious. Exclusivity. I lived the life of a royal, so I understood luxury. And I understood the way wishing to feel connected to luxury could drive some men insane. And so I cultivated that angle. I manipulated human nature. Because if there is one thing that I have learned it's that humans do not change. And that they can always be exploited for your purposes."

"So, no part of you feels passionate about the luxury travel industry?"

"Every time I walked into one of my own hotels I was very aware that my brother—if he was still alive—was being kept in appalling conditions. Every time I made a place for the wealthy to enjoy the heights of luxury, I was aware that my brother might be in chains. In many ways I was simply creating reminders. All around me, all the time. No. I do not feel passion for anything other than what I have done now. So now you know me. My story." He leveled his eyes on hers. "Now you can tell me yours."

"I love beautiful things. I always have." She looked down. "And I suppose I am a very shallow girl. For I have always liked the way beautifully cut clothing made me feel."

"Very nice. What a sound bite. Is that what you would say to the media?"

She looked up at him, her expression hard. "What does it matter?"

"You can continue to fight me, but the result will be the same. Will it make you feel better?"

"Perhaps nothing will make me feel better."

"That seems a reasonable response."

"Do you expect me to be reasonable?"

"No. I simply felt we might talk."

"I'm not a thirteen-year-old girl, Cairo. Not anymore. You can't bait me with an orange and a charming smile. We have gone beyond that."

"Can we pretend? For a moment. The last time I ever wanted to know what another person thought or felt was in that garden. And it was you. So perhaps you could indulge me for a moment."

He did not know where that moment of raw honesty had come from. He was not certain that such a thing had even existed in him before this moment.

And yet he found that it was true. Whether he could identify what it had come from or not.

She did not speak for a moment. And then she lifted her head. "Because I watched my mother have to come to terms with the fact that she married a monster. I watched her go from believing that she had a beautiful, perfect life, to being appalled by the realization of what my father had done. And she had to somehow keep her head held high. She would wake up in the morning, and she would feel... Destroyed. By what he had done to you, to me. By what he had done to us. And then she would put on the right shade of lipstick. A proper dress. A just so pair of earrings, and she would conquer the day regardless of what was going on inside of her. It was like watching a warrior suit up for battle. And I could appreciate then, the way that women wielded power when they did not have a sword. I watched my mother survive a very difficult betrayal, and whether or not you recognize that what happened hurt us too… It did. I was always interested in art and design, but the way that design could change the way my mother carried herself, the way that fashion allowed her to find some strengths, that is what propelled me in that direction. Perhaps I wanted to find some of it for myself. But at any rate I found that I was quite good at it."

"And you feel passion for it," he said.

"Yes," she said. "I do. I feel immensely passionate about seeing my work, my heart, come together like this. I worked so hard. So hard to get where I am. It's painful to leave it behind."

"And lovers?" He had not meant to ask that question, and it bit the edge of his tongue. The idea of a man putting his hands on her body… It did something to him. Twisted something in his soul. And yet, was his task not to bring her to his brother so that his brother might have her? Of course it was.

He bit down until he tasted blood.

It did not matter what he wanted.

"Why do you insist on asking me about things that do not matter? You don't care that I love fashion. And you don't care why. You don't care if I have a lover. You want only what you want. You do not care for me one bit."

"I have not been able to afford to care for a thing beyond the liberation of my country, and my brother."

"Well, what, then? What then—now that you have accomplished it?" she asked.

"I continue to fight."

And he would do so from his own cage.

Everyone had a cage.

His was to keep him away from her.

CHAPTER SIX

"Show me the desert."

"You hate the desert," he said.

"But you don't. I want to understand."

"All right, but we could get in trouble."

She knew they could. She had sensed that as their friendship deepened. As her feelings for him became more and more difficult. As it became clear to her she...

She thought he was the most beautiful boy she'd ever known, and she wanted to hate Nazul with all that she was, but she could never hate Cairo.

"I don't care," she said. "Show me."

She didn't know why she found this conversation so... Infuriating. Perhaps it was the way he pretended that he cared. The way he acted as if her feelings mattered even a little bit. When she knew they did not. He was going to do exactly what he wanted to, no matter what she said to him. There was no appealing to his better nature. That nature did not exist. *The boy that you want him to be doesn't exist.*

She had to confess, even if to herself, sitting there feeling guiltily sated from the meal that he had just put before her, that she had felt a sense of… Jealousy twisted up inside of her when she had overheard him speaking to that woman.

When she talked about Stockholm syndrome, in part, she wasn't kidding. And she didn't like it one bit.

But his raw, masculine beauty called to her. As did something about being here in the desert. She thought of the way that she had stood before the window, naked. The way that she'd felt… Thrilled by it.

And just then, she felt a surge of something wild within her.

"Would you show me the desert?"

She hadn't meant to ask that, in quite those terms. She hadn't meant to echo the conversation from that last day. Oh, that last night.

How she'd wished she'd kissed him that last night.

But she'd been fourteen. Engaged to his brother. Even if it was against her will.

Even if it had been him she'd desired.

She *didn't* want to kiss him now. She ignored the throb in her body that called her a liar.

"Excuse me?"

"I wish to tour the grounds," she said, re-phrasing. "We did once sit outside in the gardens at the palace, did we not? When I felt hopeless about the future. About my position in your country. About everything. We sat there in the blossoms, and we talked like human beings. I just… I want to go outside for a moment."

"As you wish," he said, standing and looking at her with distrust. She didn't know what she wanted, but she knew that her heart was pounding like a bird trapped in a cage. Or rather, like what she was. A woman caught in a trap.

One thing she knew… She would fight.

Because if she did not she wouldn't be able to respect herself.

It was a slow dawning realization that while her mother had always been kind to her, she had been passive. She had been passive in her own life, and in Ariel's. And Ariel feared that in many ways she'd fallen into that same passivity. Acceptance.

Her mother had accepted a husband who had decided their daughter would have a political marriage, and who knew what other red flags she'd ignored? She'd expressed sympathy for Ariel's desire to not marry Riyaz, but in the end had done nothing to stop it.

She had told Ariel to be on guard for Riyaz's return, and yet had treated it like an inevitability, and Ariel could see the echoes of this in her own life.

Yes, as a young girl she'd accepted what her father had told her but eventually she'd begun to want her own, separate things.

When she'd been bundled up to go to Nazul every year she had complained, she hadn't fought.

When she'd been fourteen, she hadn't fought. She'd wanted to kiss Cairo, and she hadn't done it. She'd wanted him and not Riyaz and she hadn't done a thing about it. It wasn't a kiss she needed now, but the spirit remained.

She did not want to marry Riyaz. She didn't want the life that had been prescribed to her, and she would fight, even knowing she couldn't win.

She would fight because it would make her something more than a captive.

She had to be brave now, where she hadn't been before.

He went behind her chair and positioned himself so that he could pull it out for her while she stood. It was such an odd thing. The way that he played the part of a gentleman even while holding her against her will.

He took her arm, as if he was a man taking her out for a night on the town, and not a walk out in the desert.

He led her back to the spacious entry, and out the front door, which only opened because of the touch of his palm.

Yes. She even needed him to get outside. She was right to try this. Right to do it.

She made a somewhat decisive move away from him as the evening air enveloped her. "It's beautiful," she said, spinning in a circle. What she had said about clothing had not been wrong. She felt powerful in this dress. She felt like the sort of woman who could do whatever she wanted. Who could bend the universe to her will.

And she would try. She would try, no matter the cost.

She looked around and took stock of her surroundings. Took another step to keep herself just distant enough.

And then thunder rolled, out there in the desert, echoing off the mountains all around them.

"What is that?"

"A storm. We shouldn't stay out here. They rage hard and fast."

One fat drop of water landed on her face. Then another. "Just a moment," she whispered.

"Ariel…"

And that was when she ran. She ran like the desert contained her salvation and she had no choice but to fling herself into it, arms wide open. Water hit against her body, cold and harsh, and she ran.

She ran, in jeweled slippers and a gown made of silk that clung to her skin. She ran even though she could not win. She ran because it was the only way she would ever be able to continue to look at herself in the mirror day in and day out for the remainder of her life, which she would no doubt spend as a prisoner.

A prisoner.

She ran. Tears streaming down her face. And when she felt a strong arm grab her around the waist, and when she found herself being spun, her back hitting firmly against the rock wall of the mountain behind her, with a wall of male muscle in front, she let out a sob of distress.

Everything in her rebelled against this moment. Against this man. Against the inevi-

tability of it. She pounded her fists against
his chest. And let out the most vile string of
curses she'd ever said in all her life.

"I hate you," she shouted. "I don't want to
be a prisoner for the rest of my life." She hit
him again, and he simply stood fast, holding
her still with ease. The storm that she un-
leashed upon him was a tiny, wrecked gull
raging against the tempest.

"I will not be a prisoner for the rest of my
life."

She shrieked it. Shouted it. Until she felt
the tide beginning to turn inside of herself.
Until she felt the power begin to turn and
shift within her.

Until she felt herself begin to change.
Until the words took on new meaning. Until
she recognized the power within them. The
power within herself. She had known that she
wouldn't escape, out here in the desert. She
had known. But she had to do it to prove her
mettle. To prove her might. To prove that she
was not a wilting flower who would go into
the heat to die, but rather a gem who would
only become stronger through fire and flame.

"I am not a prisoner," she said. "I'm Ariel
Hart. I'm a world-renowned fashion designer.
And I did not betray you. I don't deserve to
be held against my will, to have everything

that I have worked for stripped away from me. I don't deserve it, and I refuse to be punished for the sins of my father. I demand that you give me a life, or I will never stop trying to run. Because as long as I'm in a cage I will kick against the bars, I promise you that, Cairo."

"You are a fool," he hissed, moving closer to her, the rain sliding down over his handsome face. So close. So close. "You would die out here. Me capturing you is the kindest thing that could happen."

"I'm not afraid. I'm not afraid to challenge death. To challenge the desert. I have never been afraid. Always, the men around me have sought to manipulate my life. To decide who I am and what I can do and how much I can be. And only with my father gone, only with your brother in prison, was I able to pursue a life of my own. I went and made myself a success, and I had to spend those years hoping that…"

"Hoping I was dead?"

Never that.

Oh, never that.

Even standing here now, awash in her rage and indignity, she'd never want him dead.

It was the worst part of all of this. Her connection to him. The fact that she could never be fully certain if the reason she hadn't jumped out of that car back in Paris wasn't to save herself the road rash, but to give herself some time with him.

If the reason she'd run now, knowing she would be caught, was because part of her didn't want to be free of him.

"I deserve it," she said, to herself as much as him. But she didn't know now what she thought she deserved. It was tangled up in all this heat. In him. "And I will fight for it. I will not simply become your docile princess."

He gripped her hard by the shoulders, his hands biting into her. "What is it you want? Do you want the moon? Is that it?"

Ya amar.

His moon. He had called her that before. It was a memory that haunted her, for there was no other word for it. The kind of memory that kept her trapped. The kind that made it so no other man ever piqued her interest.

The kind that let him into her dreams.

"Shall I climb up there and pull it down for you?" he continued, a rough rage in his voice she didn't understand. "I cannot do that any more than I can grant you your freedom. This is a set path."

"I wish to be allowed to retain my work. I wish to have freedom. I will not be kept in a palace as a symbol. I'm more than a symbol. If this is to be my life, then this life must contain all that I desire."

"And that is?"

"My career, as I said. But I will need the freedom to travel."

"And if you escape?"

"That is simply it. I cannot be treated like a prisoner. If I'm not treated like a prisoner, perhaps I will not behave as one. But if I am, then I promise that is all you will get from me."

"What do you need here, now?"

"I need a computer. I need access to email and the internet. I need a phone. I cannot be kept away from the outside world."

"Once we get to my country. Then you may have those things. But not before then."

"If you do not trust me…"

"You just tried to run away out to the middle of the desert at night. You could've been bitten by a viper. Worse. There are jackals out here. You would make a nice meal for them."

"I told you. I'm not afraid."

"Perhaps you were not afraid because you have never seen someone die. But I have, Ariel. I fear it. I saw no peace in it."

She was silenced by that. "But you will

give me those things when we're back at the palace?"

"Yes."

"And if Riyaz does not wish for me to have these things?"

"Riyaz is having to learn how to… Be a real boy. For lack of a better way of describing it. He will acquiesce to what I tell him is appropriate."

"You are certain?"

"I will see that it is so. I told you, this is not a punishment. It is the fulfillment of what is right. I am not holding you captive."

"Am I free to go?"

"No. But you are not…in danger. No harm will come to you. My aim is not to crush you. We will continue to discuss the terms of this as we await further clarity on the situation."

And she knew that she had won a victory. She knew that the wildness of the desert, the wildness in her, the way that they echoed around and within each other, but it was the truth of who she was. That it was what she was meant to be. She had to listen to the wildness at her core.

That wildness would guide her. And it would make sure she had a life. Even if…

Her thoughts trailed off. He was still touching her. His hands on her shoulders. His face close. He was beautiful. This man who was her enemy. This man who held her captive.

And she did not mean held her captive by holding her prisoner. But rather, kept her captivated by the intensity in his dark gaze.

And it was funny that when she thought about her future, what she thought was in terms of what she might have to give up. Her career. Her freedom. Her travel. But what she could not think of was being married to Riyaz. Not only because she could not imagine the man—she hadn't seen him since he was sixteen years old. But also because... Cairo would be her brother-in-law. And Cairo might elicit inside of her a mix of reactions, but many of them were not appropriate for a man who would hold that position and title.

Had she ever been running from Cairo?

Had it only ever been Riyaz? Was that why she was here now, feeling all of these things?

"Let us go back to the house," he said.

She was soaked through to the bone now. Tired. Exhausted.

"Let go of me," she said.

"Only if you promise not to run."

And she wanted...she wanted to kiss him. Or maybe more accurately, she wanted to live a life where she *could* kiss him.

Hadn't that always been what she'd wanted?

Hadn't it always been what she was denied?

No matter whether she was fourteen and promised to his brother, a free woman in Paris promised to no one, or an escaped prisoner in the desert...

In none of those lives had kissing him ever been possible.

"I can't promise that," she whispered.

"I promise you your freedom when we get to the palace," he said, his voice rough. He moved his face even closer to hers, his lips so close, so very close. "Now promise me you will not run."

There was a heartbeat, a space, a breath, where she thought to defy him.

Or herself.

She didn't not know which.

"I won't run," she said instead.

And when he let go of her, she could swear that she saw relief in his dark gaze, and she wondered why. She would not try to run again. Not tonight. Because he was right. Because there was death out there waiting in the desert, and she did not wish to court that level of danger. Her running had not been about that. It had been about being willing. Willing to risk everything for freedom. And perhaps she would not be able to gain all of her freedom, but she would not live as a prisoner.

That would be her rallying cry. That would be her declaration.

It was clear to her, however, that whatever it was she felt burning in her now... He felt the same.

The realization made her stomach hollow itself out. And she decided there was a limit to the wildness that she would chase in the desert. She might be willing to tempt death by running out into nothingness, but she would not tempt him.

The idea made her shiver.

"Cold? Imagine how cold you would've been if you were out sleeping on the desert floor. You would not have fared well in a flash flood."

"I wouldn't have slept for long according to you. There are jackals out there. Though I suspect that there might be jackals where I'm headed too."

He grinned then, his white teeth gleaming. "If I intended to eat you, Ariel, you would know."

The hardness in his voice called to something feminine in her. The dangerous edge to his tone like a blade slicing against her tender skin. And she shivered. This time, definitely not from the cold.

"When you say that Riyaz is not well..."

"We will not discuss him tonight." They arrived back at the house, and he allowed her entry. There was a mirror just at the entry, and she looked at it and saw herself. Her hair askew, her makeup having run down her face. She looked a misery. And she had imagined that there had been something like heat between them back there. The idea was laughable. If the clothing had felt like her armor only an hour ago, it felt like a costume now. Not fitting of the bedraggled, ruined creature that stood there looking in the mirror now.

"I need to sleep," she said.

"I'm glad that you finally think so. You had a long day."

"Yes."

And as the years stretched on in front of her, she wondered if every day would feel this long.

And when she looked at Cairo, the feeling that was created inside of her was more confusing than she would like to admit.

"Change into dry clothes," he said. "And sleep. For in the morning, we must begin to see to your education."

And as she watched him walk away, his clothes clinging to him because of the rain—yet he looked no less imposing for it—she realized she would comply.

Because Cairo needed this.

And one thing she had never been able to turn away from was him.

She wasn't choosing Riyaz.

But part of her was choosing Cairo.

Or perhaps had chosen him all those years ago in Nazul.

Perhaps what really held her here was not the vastness of the desert or the power of the al Hadid family.

But feelings for Cairo that had grown like orange blossoms in the unforgiving sun when she had been far too young to fear their power.

CHAPTER SEVEN

SHOW ME THE DESERT...

He cursed himself as a fool for the entire rest of the night. The memory of her skin beneath his hands...

He never should've let her go outside. He never should've let her get in a position to run. Less still, should he have negotiated with her.

Weakness.

Ariel Hart had always been an unforgivable weakness.

It was time for breakfast now, and the spread of pastries and very strong coffee that was laid out on the table was mocked by the fact that she had not arrived on time as he had bid her to. If she had run again in the night...

But the house was locked up, and you could only get out if your palm print matched those programmed into the security system. So she could not have done so.

You are soft for her. You always have been.

He gritted his teeth. He was not a stupid boy anymore.

He would not be. It was unacceptable. He would not be soft for the woman, because there was no room for softness in him. In his life. In this world.

Finally, she appeared. She was wearing a pair of high waisted olive green pants with safari pockets and a white shirt. Her hair was tied low on her neck, a white silk scarf holding it back. She looked simple, with no makeup on her face. And yet she made everything in him go tight. And he remembered what she had said last night. About her mother. About armor. About the way clothing made her feel as if she had the strength to face down what she must. He could see how it was true now for her. Could see the way that she had dressed herself today, quite different from last night. Last night her clothing had been a distraction. Glittery, sensual.

Today, they were a riff on the masculine. Much more no nonsense. She had come to negotiate today. Not distract him with her body, and yet, distracted he remained.

"Good of you to join me."

"Apologies. I found that I rather took longer in the bath than intended. It is a beautiful bath."

And her words force the image into his mind of her naked body gliding through the water.

Lust kicked him, square and hard. He could not believe that she had chosen her words by accident.

But why? Why would she choose to goad him like this? Was he the only one remembering the past, or did their shared memories haunt her too?

He had to accept the idea that he might be reading something into their interaction. Something he had never done in his life. Not even once. When a woman wanted him, he knew.

"I'm not sure what you intend to teach me," she said, sitting down at the table and reaching out, piling pastries onto her plate before grabbing the coffee pot and pouring herself a measure of strong, dark liquid.

She took a sip, took a bite of croissant, then sighed.

"You seem an entirely different woman than the one I left last night."

"A mental breakdown can do wonders for the spirit. Sometimes giving into despair is the beginning of fighting your way back up."

"Funny, I'm not sure I trust you."

She shrugged, then licked some sugar off her finger. He felt the action echo along his length and nearly cursed out loud.

This was unconscionable.

He could not want her. She was for Riyaz. Riyaz, who would have to be tamed into something much more civilized before he could ever go near her. Riyaz who... It was entirely possible that Riyaz had not touched a woman in sixteen years. And then... Given his age when he was taken into the dungeon... It was entirely possible he never had. He looked at Ariel, and he wondered what that might mean for her. If that would mean a brutal, unpracticed experience for her.

She was a beautiful woman. Undoubtedly she'd had her share of lovers. He could only hope that her skill would compensate for the lack of it potentially found in Riyaz. He did his best not to think of it. "I'm asking you again," she said, "what is it you intend to teach me? Because you know that I was schooled in the customs of your country from the time I was a child. I spent summers there. I learned the language. I have been in training to be the sheikha for years. So what is it that..."

"There were things you were never taught.

You had not been walked through the customs that would be present at the wedding. The dance. It is important that you know. It is important that you walk in armed. Is it not?"

And he wondered who this was for.

This was education Riyaz would be doing if he was not being put back together. And so… He would do this. She was afraid. She did not want to lose everything. She did not want to leave it all behind. That was understandable. He would see her well prepared to go toe to toe with his brother. To be the bride at the spectacle of a wedding that they would be throwing. The wedding that would signal their true return to power. The sheikh is dead. Long live the sheikh.

"I didn't realize…"

"There is a maze of customs to navigate. And strengthening the customs of the nation is part of my sworn duty. Showing them that all is well. The wedding must go off without a hitch."

"You are truly not used to anything opposing you."

"Very rarely has anything tried. Except you."

"So I'm to get princess lessons?"

"It is more than that. You are correct. You cannot live as a prisoner. It will not do. You must be strong, you must be traditional, a symbol of all that was good, and a symbol of all that is now better."

"How nice for me. And what do you get to be a symbol of, Cairo?"

"Endurance. Of never giving up. Hope. While Riyaz is a symbol of our strength. He is not broken. Not truly. I will not allow that to be so."

He couldn't let it be the end of his brother. The truth of him. If Riyaz was broken beyond repair then Cairo's life didn't matter at all.

"You love him."

"I always have. He is my older brother. My idol. My future king. When we were younger… He had both everything and nothing that I wanted."

He realized the words could not make sense to her. But it was true. He had never envied Riyaz's duty. Not ever. He had envied him Ariel. But that was all. Yes. He had envied him Ariel. But mostly… He had simply admired his older brother. Seen him as a great and glorious leader. And the best older brother. Strong. Intelligent. Quick with it. He had seen Riyaz but briefly in the time since he had been extracted from the dungeon. He spoke with no concept of what was appropriate and what was not. It seemed at times he lived to be deliberately provocative, and yet he could see there was nothing so calculated in his brother. He acted on animal instinct. And there were rages…

Yes. The rages.

"I will lay down my life to protect him," Cairo said. "Already, I have sacrificed many years to protect him. I will continue to do so."

"It's quite sad," she said suddenly, her eyes going vacant.

"What is?"

"I don't have anyone in my life I feel that way about. I'm defending my… My business. I love my business. I love what I do. I'm so very passionate about it. But it was not piecing a country back together. I'm angry at you, Cairo. But I cannot deny that you have done more with your life than I have with mine. In sheer terms of what you have given to others. Every employee that I have met is slavishly devoted to you, and it is because of what you've done for them. And then you really mean it. You're giving everything for Riyaz. And I was weeping in the desert over my fashion label."

"It is a gift," he said slowly, "to have such dreams, Ariel. A gift to be allowed to want things. You should not feel ashamed."

His own desires were not allowed.

"I think I understand you better now. My mother… She might be my style icon. But… We are not close. Not really. What happened with my father was too difficult. She was heartbroken by his actions. They separated. And then he died. And it was all just awful. Layers upon layers of heartbreak. For what? So that he could have money and power. He did not love us more than that." She took a shuddering breath. "And then he died. He didn't even get to spend the money. Not much of it. He died without family. I think my mother felt broken by that. Truly. To where even spending time with me became painful. Because I reminded her of the time that was spent in your country. Of my father's pursuits. Of that which became more important than us. And the lives of your family. Riyaz has been in a dungeon for the last fifteen years, and I think that you still may have a stronger bond with him than I do with my mother."

"It is a tragedy. All around. On every front. But I will see it restored."

"When do these lessons begin?" She finished her cup of coffee and poured herself another.

"Now."

"Please do let me finish my coffee."

"You can bring it with you."

Her eyes flickered, but the corners of her mouth turned upward. "I don't see a to-go cup."

"Bring the fine china. Much more eco-friendly than a disposable cup anyway.

Her heart was racing. There was something about the conversation they'd just had that set her alight. And now she was being ushered into a massive room with windows floor to ceiling, with the promise that Cairo would be with her shortly.

It was early yet, so the sun wasn't half as punishing is it would become later. She could see the bright and arid desert below, and something began to throb between her thighs. Shame ignited within her, and she looked back and saw Cairo, and the feeling intensified. She'd had a host of erotic dreams last night. The kinds of images that had never plagued her before. Not once.

It was unendurable. Maybe it was because the specter of the fact that she would...

That she would presumably be sleeping with Riyaz loomed over her head.

She knew about sex. She was a woman in the world, after all. She worked in an industry that was practically saturated in sexuality. Naked models were always strewn about backstage off the catwalks, and she did fittings on beautiful people in every position along the gender spectrum all the time. She simply didn't react to it. It was part of work. Meanwhile, they were all sleeping with each other in various combinations, and seemed to take it quite casually. Ditto the commentary on it. She was often treated to graphic details about somebody's sexual exploits.

And yet, it had remained theoretical for her. She had attributed it to early trauma and all of that. The fact that she had been bound to a man that she didn't choose from the time she was a child. Oh, yes, she had given herself a great many reasons for why her sexuality was just a little bit dampened.

Except she was beginning to wonder if that was the case. Or if it had simply gone into hiding until she could see Cairo again.

Because she still remembered that day. That sun-drenched day in the desert...

Was that why even the desert aroused her?

Was it because of him? That was the most disturbing thought she'd ever had.

She heard decisive footsteps behind her and she turned to see Cairo step into the room. "It is a good view," he said.

"Yes. A great view of the landscape that wants to kill me."

"It doesn't want to kill you. It doesn't think of you at all. But if you were to walk into its jaws, it would not hesitate to swallow you whole."

There was something about those words. Something about the way they landed. Like a pomegranate seed at the center of her chest. And then it began to expand. As if it was growing into an entire tree. Blossoming inside of her, twisting and divining throughout her entire body. She felt invaded. By his words. By his scent. By his presence. "The wedding ceremony in Nazul lasts for three days. The bride and groom meet one another at the altar, and they extend their hands."

Without thinking, she moved her right hand forward.

"Not your right," he said. "The left. That is the hand for making vows. Unbreakable promises." He reached out with his left hand and took hers. He turned his palm slightly, then wrapped his fingers around hers, and reflexively she did the same. Then with his right hand he took a silken scarf from his pocket. "When the bride and groom take hands like this, their hands are then tethered together."

She remembered this. The silk scarf. Red and brilliant, behind the display of wedding jewelry he had shown her at the palace.

She'd been hurt that he'd shown it to her.

She'd felt like he was reminding her that she was marrying Riyaz.

And not him.

But now he was standing before her, holding the scarf. And she couldn't breathe. "It is symbolic of the fact that the words that you speak will bind you," he continued. "That even if you release your hold, it is those words that hold you there. The bride and groom do not kiss. They speak vows, the scarf is tied. And then..." He reached out and pressed his thumb against her forehead. "With your thoughts." Then his thumb slid down to her lips, and her breath caught. "With your words." And then down yet again to the center of her breasts. Her breath froze. "With your heart. Serve me only."

"I..."

"And then you."

She took her hand and lifted it to his forehead, but she realized that her fingers were trembling. "With your thoughts. With your words." She could not bring herself to make full contact with his mouth. But then he grabbed her hand and pressed her palm flat over his chest. "With your heart. Serve only me."

And she felt changed. It was an awful feeling. Terrifying. And there was nothing that she could do about it. She felt as if she had made vows to him. In this very room. And when she looked up and looked into his eyes… Her breath seemed to freeze in her chest altogether. It was more intimate than a kiss.

At least she imagined it was. She had never been kissed.

She wondered now for the first time if it was because of the kiss she'd never given him. If her body was still waiting for it.

She swallowed hard and pulled away, the silk scarf around their hands unraveling as she did. "Those are very interesting vows."

"I have always thought they were romantic. My parents were in love. Very much."

"Then why did they arrange a marriage for Riyaz?"

"Their marriage was arranged," said Cairo. "Love followed. They believed that was the path to love."

"Oh."

"For them it resulted in the greatest love imaginable, so why would they consider another way for their children? They saw it as a sort of fate."

"I see." Except she didn't, and her whole body still burned.

"After that there is the feast. It will be outside in a big tent that includes the entirety of the palace. All families. Regardless of wealth and status. Food will be brought out to the villages as well. The celebration will be spread everywhere. For everyone. It is a wedding. And weddings are about abundance. Abundance of joy. Abundance of food."

"And after the food?"

"Let us worry about it tomorrow. Tonight… we will have a feast."

CHAPTER EIGHT

"THE DESERT AT night is beautiful."

She looked at him instead of the moon and the stars. She looked at him like he was the moon and the stars.

"I told you that it was. Not as hot. But dangerous. You have to be careful. You cannot come out here alone."

She clung to his arm, and he felt a rising tide of desire. It frightened him. He was not a stranger to sexual arousal. But he had never felt that for another person. Not like this. Not while he was with them. "I wouldn't. I promise. I won't do anything dangerous, Cairo. I wouldn't want to be out here without you anyway."

She smiled up at him. And the moon made her face glow. She had never asked why he called her his moon. Because in the desert, in the dark, on a clear night, a full moon was a gift. It could light your way. Guide you. That was what she felt like to him. She felt like far too much. Far too special. Far too important. She could be his friend. They could always be friends. Of course they could. But she would marry Riyaz someday. And he would not be able to walk alone with her. He would not be able to touch her.

And he found himself reaching out then to touch her face. "Ariel," he said, her name a whisper when he didn't mean it to be.

Her eyes went round and glassy, and they reflected the stars. As if she was made of them.

"Cairo," she whispered.

He wanted to kiss her. But he knew that he couldn't. Not ever. He should not have ever showed her those gems. He should never have let himself think about putting them on her body. He should never have allowed himself to dream, even for a moment, about binding her to him.

It was forbidden.

She had been told to dress for a feast. A wedding feast. Apparently, she was being prepared for what would happen on day two of the wedding.

The idea made her uneasy. She dressed in a pink gown tonight. With long billowing sleeves and glimmering turquoise jewels sewn into the fabric. It swished when she walked, a mermaid shaped gown with a high waist.

It covered almost every inch of skin. And yet, it revealed the shape of her figure in a way that made her feel… Well. She felt quite sexy, and she'd never given much thought to how she felt about her own appearance. Not really.

When she walked into the dining room, he was not there. But Aisha was.

"He is waiting for you outside in the garden."

"Oh," she said.

"I will show you."

Of course, Aisha would have to show her, because she knew she couldn't exit any part of the palace without an approved palm print. She had tried.

But then, she didn't feel all that inspired to try to run again. Not after…

She thought of what happened last night. Running in the rainstorm. Fighting against him like that. He was a strong, solid wall of muscle. A strong, solid wall of man. There was no running from him. No opposing him. Not really.

Aisha pressed her palm to a doorway she

hadn't gone through before, and it opened. There was a garden back here. Landscaped and beautiful, surrounded entirely by the mountain. Private. It was lit up now, even in the darkness. Glowing mosaic lights casting colorful sunspots everywhere. The ground was tiled in white and blue, and there was a fountain at the center. And fruit trees. Like the palace in Nazul. Like the palace where she and Cairo had sat together. And there he was. Wearing a white shirt tucked into black pants. The shirt was unbuttoned midway down his chest, and she could not help but admire his stark, tanned skin, and the contrast with the pale fabric. He looked strong and beautiful. Vital.

She swallowed hard. Everything had felt upside down from the moment he had come back into her life. He had kidnapped her after all. Turned everything a different way.

It had also been like he'd returned from the dead. She had always hoped that he lived. But she hadn't known. And for the first time, she allowed herself to feel a rush of gratitude that the boy she had cared so much for was still alive. Even if he had grown into a man whose purposes opposed her own.

He said he wouldn't make you a prisoner.
And maybe she had to accept that as a com-

promise. Except, of course some women got to live their entire lives in freedom.

You've had over fifteen years of freedom. And you built a wonderful business with it. But what have you done with your personal life?

She had never been in love with anyone. Not anyone but him.

She ignored that treacherous thought. It wasn't that she was in love with him... Maybe she had thought that she was. And maybe it had kept her from moving on. Even now, his masculine beauty left her speechless. Even now it appealed to her in a way that no one else ever had.

He was so strong and solid, and she was torn between wanting to fling herself at him and hit him again like she had done last night. And... Throw herself at him and cling to him. To move her hand over that flash of bare skin of his chest. To feel his muscles, the heat of his skin, his chest hair.

She blinked, and then turned to look at Aisha, but the other woman had melted away, leaving her there alone with Cairo.

"This is the feast that we will have for the wedding," he said, gesturing to a table behind him. She hadn't even looked at the table. She had been so focused on him.

So focused on the reality that what she had done with her freedom had been… Very, very limited. All this time she could have done whatever she wanted. Taken whichever lover she chose. She hadn't. Because a part of her had never left Nazul. Whatever she told herself, a part of her had never been truly free, and it wasn't simply a matter of waiting for Riyaz to escape the dungeon. It was something deeper than that. Much, much deeper.

Something she couldn't bear to examine. Not now.

"Come, my moon. Have a seat." He held the chair out for her. It was a glorious chair. Golden mosaic like everything else in the garden. And she found herself obeying his command, taking her seat at the table. "Spiced lamb," he said. "Couscous with mint. Lemon rice. These will be the traditional things you will find at your wedding feast."

"I see."

There was a cake as well, at his end of the table.

"What is the cake?"

"Saffron. Honey and orange."

Orange. The tang of it settled on her tongue even without having tasted it. The promise of it.

And it reminded her of that day in the garden. And this reminded her of that night long ago.

When he had touched her cheek. They had very nearly kissed that night. She had always been sure of it. The idea had often terrified her. Because she had wondered... Though they were young... She had wondered if Cairo would have ever actually touched his mouth to hers if they would have ever been able to stop at a kiss. Or if passion would have carried them to a place where the consequences might have been far-reaching for her. Especially since... Days after that night she had left. And then his family was gone.

She began to serve herself food, trying her best to banish thoughts from long ago.

"How did you find out when it happened?"

She looked up at him, his dark gaze measured there from across the table.

"My father told us. He told my mother and I as if we should be proud. He knew that I had never wanted to marry Riyaz, so he thought that I would... Celebrate. That he had gotten money for betraying your parents. For helping their enemies figure out how to get into the palace. For helping them find their weakness. We were both... Horrified."

She remembered throwing herself to the ground and weeping until she could not breathe. She hadn't wanted to marry Riyaz. She hadn't been happy there in Nazul. But the sheikh and sheikha had never been anything but kind to her, and Riyaz, though serious and distant, had never been an object of hatred for her.

But it was Cairo. The thought of Cairo, bleeding on the mosaic tile that had broken her.

"I asked about you. My father said that no one had ever found your body. But that you were presumed dead. Cairo, I…"

"Your father was shocked that you and your mother did not praise his perfidy?"

"Yes. And I think even more shocked when my mother left him over it. He had thought that money was what she wanted. It wasn't. I know that my father understood loyalty. I don't think he understood love. My mother could not stay with a man who had caused so much pain. And I… I could never look at him again." *I felt like I died that day with you.*

But she did not say that last part out loud.

Instead, she looked down at her plate, and then back up at him. "How did you escape?"

"It wasn't easy. There was a battle. Intense and bloody. My mother was killed. My father raised his sword to fight. And he took down many of the men who invaded the palace. Before he died, he whispered to me that I had to survive. That I had to run. He said they had not killed Riyaz but that he had been taken prisoner. Sometimes I... Over the years, I wondered if he had lied to me. If he had told me that to keep me from staying and dying. If he had given me a mission as a gift. It was a despairing thought. I needed to believe that my brother lived. But there were persistent rumors that he was a prisoner. And I hoped in those rumors."

"But how did you escape?"

"It was a melee. I knew a secret entrance out to the gardens. I slipped away in the fighting and got free of the palace. There were soldiers—enemy soldiers—stationed in the garden, but... You remember the orange tree."

"Yes." Of course she did.

"I climbed the tree to escape over the wall."

"But what was out there beyond the wall?"

"The desert. When I speak to you of the harsh sun, the jackals, of flash floods and freezing nights, it is because I have survived in the desert. I walked until I escaped over the border into Turkey. And from there I was able to gain safe passage to England as a refugee. There were many people who left Nazul around that time. By the time I arrived there, I was unrecognizable as Cairo. I had lost so much weight and was chapped and weathered from the sun. There was a man who gave me fake papers. Syed. The name that you had seen in the media. That was when I adopted that name. That is how I escaped."

"It sounds… Awful."

"It was. It was only the thought of Riyaz that kept me going. For a great number of years. And then… I went to school, and I made friends. I started my own business and began to earn money. I of course discovered pleasures of the flesh. And the pleasures of alcohol. I was… Rudderless for a time. And I will not say that I am proud of everything that I did. I felt that there was no reason to leave any stone unturned when it came to substances or sex. It was like a delayed response to surviving the massacre. A celebration of being alive. Or perhaps a punishment to my body for doing so. And then gradually I became adept at figuring out how to work my way toward staging the next coup for Nazul and pleasing myself. I became quite good at the balance."

It was funny, for even though she felt as if she had left desire and attraction behind in Nazul along with him, and even though she had not done the same thing he had, it felt much like the same. For the way he talked about sex was as if it were a self-medication of some kind. Not so much about desire as it was about the need to blot out unfortunate memories. It didn't sound like pleasure.

Not really.

He spoke of it as if it were any sort of drug.

And she wondered what other damage had been done to him. Wondered what else had scarred his soul. Changed the course of who he was. Because the fact was...

She might have escaped her betrothal to Riyaz, but she had never really escaped Nazul.

They finished eating, and then were brought a fresh pot of coffee to go alongside the cake.

The staff melted away again, leaving them alone. And suddenly, it did not feel like a rehearsal for anything. It simply felt like she was out in the desert at night with Cairo. Much like that night when they had been teenagers.

Her body ached with it.

She looked up at him, and pain bloomed in her chest.

Pain for what he had been through. Pain for what he had lost. Pain for what the two of them had lost. For they both had lost something that day.

He picked up the cake, and moved around the table, coming to sit in the chair beside her, and she found her breath freezing at the base of her throat. He pushed his fork into the end of the cake and brought it up to her lips. "Try it."

His eyes never left hers as she parted her lips slowly and took the cake inside. As the sharp, citrusy flavor burst on her tongue. It felt intimate. Sitting this close to him while tasting the decadence of the dessert. The moon was bright. And the stars shone with vibrance. And then he reached out and touched her cheek.

"Cairo," she whispered.

He had made a mistake. This was a dangerous game. He should not have brought the meal outside…he should not have set this up at all. Princess lessons? She did not need to practice eating dinner. And yet… He had felt that he wanted to do this. For her. With her. He could not quite credit it. Could not quite figure out what he had been thinking, except he had felt compelled to give her something.

Her breakdown in the desert, and then the tension the following day when he had bound the scarf around her hands…

It was like when they were young. And

he had felt compelled to give her something nice. To make up for the fact that she was somewhere she did not wish to be. Except now was he not the captor? Except now was he not the one who had brought her here? Not her father, but him. He was her jailer in many respects, and he had no right to think that he could bribe her with cake to make it all better when what she wanted was to return to Paris. But there was no question of that, any more than there was a question of...

His chest went tight.

She looked up at him, and he saw the stars in her eyes. And he remembered. Remembered what it was like all those years ago when he had looked down at her and seen...

Hope. A future. One that he could not have, but one that he was desperate for all the same. The need to kiss her now was almost unendurable.

But she belongs to Riyaz.

Riyaz had demanded her. Payment for his suffering.

The bride price. The daughter of his enemy.

Satisfaction for that which he had endured.

For that which Cairo bore blame.

How could he touch her?

She was here because he was bound to do

what Riyaz had asked. Because he had to deny himself.

But in this moment he could not look at her and see that. She was simply Ariel. As he had seen her then. The gown she wore showed none of her pale, enticing skin, and yet he was bewitched by it. By the way the fabric clung to her curves. By the way it revealed the shape of her body. He ached. When he had been a boy, he had no practice restraining himself, but he had no knowledge of what touching a woman entailed either.

He knew now. He also should have better restraint.

And yet he found the knowledge far outweighed any self-control he might have acquired in the last few years.

So he touched her face, moved his fingertips over her lips. Her eyes fluttered closed.

"Cairo," she whispered. He leaned in, slowly. Slowly, for he wanted to prolong the moment. Prolong the breath before the sin. And just as he stopped, a breath before her lips her eyes opened. And his world was filled with aqua stars, and it was as if a shard of glass had been pressed into his heart and turned hard. It was painful, being this close to her. "I wonder," he whispered, "if you might taste of orange."

And then he curved his hand around the back of her head and closed the distance between their mouths.

She was citrus and softness and years of longing. She was the innocence of a kiss between two teenagers, and the carnal knowledge of a kiss between two adults who knew full well that what they were doing was wrong.

And he could not stop. He angled his head, deepened it, parted her lips beneath his own and slid his tongue against hers.

She gasped, and it gave him the opportunity to gain yet more ground. To take it deeper.

"Cairo," she moaned.

"Ariel. *Ya amar.*" He kissed her deeper. Harder. His body straining against the confines of his pants. His need like a dark, driving force.

He wanted her.

He wanted to strip her naked there beneath the moon. A pagan sacrifice to his selfish desires.

He wanted her.

Bring back Ariel Hart. She is what I want. She is what I'm owed.

It was Riyaz's voice, echoing in his head that brought him back from the brink. He pulled away from her, his breath ragged. Painful. "No," he said. "No. This is not possible. You are my brother's."

"I am not your brother's," she said. "I never have been. I'm my own, Cairo."

"No. You are the payment for your father's betrayal. You are the satisfaction of what was done to my family. Riyaz has demanded it, and he will have it. And if you think that you can turn my head with a kiss, you are sadly mistaken. I have had more lovers than you can count. Do you think you can tempt me? Do you think you can distract me?"

"Clearly I can," she said, her face blank.

"I'm sure you've manipulated men with your body in the past. It is a lovely body. A lovely mouth. But I am not one of those men. My honor demands that I fulfill what my brother has asked. And I will see it done. Pleas from your mouth, and cries of pleasure from your lips, will not deter me from my goal."

"Cairo," she shouted as he stood up.

He turned to face her.

"Is that what you think? That I'm trying to manipulate you?"

"Why would I? Perhaps you always were. Perhaps you always sought to use me to escape from your engagement to my brother."

"I thought we were friends. Then. Back then I thought we were friends."

"Perhaps we were. I cannot remember back that long. I cannot remember being quite so innocent."

"Maybe the years have not jaded me in the same way they have you. Maybe I didn't go out and take every lover available to me. Maybe…" Her words became rough, and he could see tears in her eyes. "Maybe I never forgot you. Did you ever think of that?" He turned away from her, turned away from the guilt that was twisting his chest. And he went back into the house, leaving her outside.

If she ran…

She wouldn't run. Somehow, he knew she wouldn't run.

He went into his study, took out his phone and called Brianna. "How is he?"

"Cairo…"

"How is he?"

"He is… Demanding. Uncivilized. Rough."

He thought of all those things being directed at Ariel.

As if you've treated her any better.

"He hasn't hurt you," he said to Brianna.

"No," she said quickly. "No, he hasn't hurt me. I don't think he would…"

"And what about Ariel? Do you think he would hurt her?"

"He thinks that she is his… Compensation. I don't think that he would hurt her."

"You're telling me you think it's safe for me to bring her back?" he asked through gritted teeth.

"You might give it a couple of days. But soon." There was a strange note to Brianna's voice, but he could not read it.

"I need to ask you something else about my brother. Do you know if they…? Has he spoken to you about his time in the dungeon?"

"Yes. Quite distinctly."

"And did he tell you whether or not they brought him women?"

"I…"

"Did they bring him women while he was in the dungeon?"

"No. They didn't."

"Thank you."

"Why did you…"

"I simply want to know what I'm bringing her into."

There was a long pause. "What is your relationship to her, Cairo?"

"That is absolutely none of your business," he said.

He hung up abruptly, her words echoing in

his ears, the softness of her kiss impressed upon his mouth.

They had not brought women to his brother while he was in the dungeon. That meant… Unless he'd supplied himself with lovers since he had been released…

It was possible, but unlikely that he would have heard. If his brother had begun bringing a parade of sex workers into the house, it was quite likely that Brianna would have mentioned it. Likely that it would have signified.

And he worried about what it might mean for Ariel. If Riyaz would have any idea how to please a woman.

Do you worry how you just hate the idea of any other man's hands on her?

It did not matter what he liked or didn't like. She belonged to Riyaz. He had made a promise. And he had to keep it.

No matter how enticing she was.

No matter that he had given in to temptation in a way that he had not done even when he'd been a boy.

But his chest still felt like it was full of glass. And he did not know what could be done about it.

CHAPTER NINE

HER LIPS STILL felt swollen the next morning. She touched them before she moved. She was lying cocooned in the large bed in her room, covered by velvet blankets. The desert sun had risen, the open windows allowing the light to pour in. But it might as well have been night, out in the garden, for all that her body still burned with Cairo's touch. She didn't understand how he affected her so. And she could not...

She was all bound up in this. In this confusion. In the desire to touch him again, kiss him again. In the knowledge that he was sending her off to marry his brother in spite of this connection between them.

And somewhere in all of that was her freedom, a distant, hazy memory.

Her life in Paris before Cairo had taken her. Before he had stormed back into her life. Why did she feel more free in his arms than she ever had at any other time in her life? She wasn't free. She was a prisoner. She was being forced to live this life. Being forced to...

Her heart was pounding hard. She got out of bed and opened up her closet, looked inside of it. She took out another white shirt, and a pair of khaki high waist pants. She'd gone for that specific Katherine Hepburn look yesterday, and she was happy to repeat it today. The sensuality of the dress from the night before... Yeah. She didn't want that feeling. Not again.

She carried the clothes into the bathroom with her and filled the tub. She looked out on the desert, naked. And the same sensual promise that she felt the first time whispered over her skin.

The thing that scared her the most was that even if she were to escape now... What was there to go back to? A career, yes. Though, Cairo had made it sound as if it was all right for her to carry on her career even as the sheikha. But she wasn't sure that she was the same person. When Cairo had so abruptly disappeared out of her life it was like a thread had been cut. And she had been set on a new path, the severing of that past connection painful and abrupt. And now it was as if she had gotten a chance to pick that thread up again, golden and beautiful, and see who she might have been if she had kept moving along it. Except… It wouldn't have been Cairo that she kissed. She would have married Riyaz. A man she couldn't even picture now. She wondered what the face of that taciturn boy looked like now that he was a man. A man that had spent the last sixteen years in a cage.

But Cairo was all she could see. Cairo was all she could want. Her heart throbbed.

Was he her enemy anymore? She wasn't sure. He wanted something for her that she didn't want for herself. But within that, he wanted her.

And that was something she simply didn't know what to do with.

She bathed herself, her skin perfumed by oils in the water. And then she got dressed, putting her hair in a low bun before heading down to breakfast. He wasn't there. She sat at the table by herself and wondered if they actually would have a lesson today, or if he would avoid her after the kiss.

The kiss. It had scalded her from the inside out.

She ate quickly, and caffeinated, and then went into the room where they had said those vows yesterday. And there he was. Standing with his back to her, looking out of the win-

dow. An echo of what she had just done up-
stairs. An echo that made her body tremble.

"And what is the lesson today?"

He turned, and the impact of his glory left
her breathless. His features were sharp, his
brows straight and dark. His nose like a blade.
His lips… They had done inestimable damage already.

"Dancing," he said.

She looked at him, and she nearly laughed.
Because the idea of him dancing seemed
absurd. He seemed twice as likely—even
dressed in his custom cut suit—as he was
to pull out a sword and start a battle. But
he reached out his hand yet again. And she
thought that if she had to touch him one more
time she would be burned.

She did not know how she could go on.
Then, he was taking her hand again.

"It is similar to dances you may have seen
or done. It is on a three count. Something like
Latin dance."

"All the dances will be like this?"

"No. But the important dance is that which
takes place between you and Riyaz. Your
groom."

"Right. My groom."

He wrapped his arm around her, with one
hand firmly clasped. And they were sud-

denly pressed tightly together. Her breasts
to his chest. His eyes didn't leave hers. And
he began to slowly count. "One. Two. Three."

And with that count came movements.
Slow but decisive. A pause, then a turn. "One.
Two. Three." The slow decisive turn carried
them swiftly over the tiled floor. She could
not remember the last time she had danced
with anyone. Maybe she never had. Maybe it
just felt like she should have. She hadn't had a
normal childhood. She hadn't gone to school
dances. Not even after her parents divorced.
Not even after the engagement to Riyaz had
presumably ended with his captivity.

This was the first time she had ever been
danced with. And while she had touched men
during garment fittings. It wasn't the same
as this.

This was Cairo.

The only man to ever hold her in his arms.

The only man to ever kiss her.

And it took her a moment to fully realize,
but she suddenly had the sense for what this
dance mimicked. The movement, the rhythm.

It was like lovers.

A husband and wife. Consummating. Coming together. How could that be? Such an intimate promise to make before all those people.

And yet, she supposed it was as old as time.

Hadn't they hung sheets out the window to prove the woman's virginity back in medieval times?

The thought of a sheet bearing her blood being suspended from a window made her wish she were dead. But then, she imagined that her inexperience with the rhythm just now betrayed her as a blood spot would. Just the same.

Abruptly, he ended the dance. Abruptly, they stopped moving. "Yes. Just like that." He stepped away from her, and he seemed to take her breath with him.

"And then what?"

"Then the bride and groom depart the festivities."

"You said that the wedding lasts three days."

"Yes. It does. But of course…the marriage must be consummated. Otherwise, it is not legal. That night, after the vows ceremony and the dance, the bride and groom depart to consummate."

"I'm sorry… You… Are you going to hang a sheet out the window with my virgin's blood on it as well?"

"What?"

"You heard me."

"I do not think that in this day and age anyone would suspect that a modern, beautiful woman such as yourself to be a virgin. Also, no. As it is not the Middle Ages."

He really didn't know? Even after the dance… He didn't know. She had sort of imagined that he might… Watch her. Have observed something of her life while he was keeping tabs on her. But apparently not. If so, he might know that she never entertained any men. That she didn't have lovers.

"So I'm simply to go off with a stranger… I have not seen Riyaz in sixteen years. And I'm supposed to show up at the palace, ready for a wedding, ready to consummate…"

Panic was beginning to swell in her breast, and she could feel herself going beyond sanity. "I hardly need princess lessons, Cairo. What I could use are lessons on how exactly I'm supposed to cope with that. How exactly I'm supposed to cope with the idea that I'm going to go from having only been kissed just once to…"

Everything around them went still. His expression was flat, his eyes dark. There was a fire in them that nearly terrified her. It wasn't like anything else she had ever seen.

This stillness. She realized what it reminded her of then. A predator. Lying in wait in the grass. Waiting for its prey to make the wrong move. Or perhaps the right move.

"You what?"

"Don't make me repeat it. I'm not ashamed of it. Nor am I embarrassed. But the reality is you are teaching me... Pomp and circumstance. All of these things are for show, the ceremony. And I am expected to... To have another person inside of me. Someone that I don't even know. I don't... I have never..."

He reached out, his hand grabbing hold of her chin, his touch was scalding. "Are you telling me that you are a virgin?"

"It's not like I go around thinking of myself that way," she said. "But it is becoming more and more difficult to avoid the word. Given that I am suddenly, very suddenly faced with the reality of what is before me."

"You have only kissed a man once?"

"Last night," she said, her whole body hot.

"Do you not like men?"

"No, that isn't it. It's just that it hasn't... I have not had the desire. Or...found the person who..."

"Forgive me. But I do not understand. You see, opportunity for me has always been quite present, and desire never short."

"Well, that's you. That isn't how it works

for me. I don't know what to tell you. I've never..."

She couldn't tell him. She could not tell him that there was a bright and warm day that lived in her mind where he had handed her a piece of fruit, and it had felt like the world had gone still. Where he had stared at her, and she had understood for the first time what it meant to be attracted to another person.

And that nothing that had ever occurred since then had matched it. How could she tell him that? Especially when it wasn't true for him. He'd slept with everything. Everything that moved. That was what the tabloids said, that was the impression that he had given.

The moment had not meant to him what it did to her, so why indulge herself by thinking of it? And why admit to him that it mattered at all?

"This could be a problem," he said.

"Why? I would've thought that you would crow about it. I mean, doesn't it complete the whole barbarian trophy, being brought back to your king? A virgin at that."

"You know how to please yourself?"

"I..." Her mouth dropped open, and then snapped back shut. Suddenly, a pulse began to beat hard between her legs.

"Do you know how to please yourself?"

His voice became dark, slick. Coated in honey. It made her tremble. Made her entire body feel weak. They should not be talking about this. Except… Who was here to make such rules? He was in charge.

He was in charge.

"I have not… I have not given enough thought to it to explore that particular…"

"You have not brought yourself to orgasm?"

"No."

And for the first time she was forced to confront how deeply she had shut down that part of herself. Perhaps it was because of the arranged marriage. Perhaps it was because of her father's betrayal of the person she was supposed to marry. Perhaps it was thinking Cairo was dead.

She didn't know, because she had not pondered it overly much, because it was… Distressing. Tangled around this trauma in her past that she had wanted to pretend wasn't trauma at all. She had wanted to pretend that she had gone on to be successful and that was all that mattered. That she was fine. That all was well.

And yet she could see that it wasn't. That it never had been.

"This could very well be a problem."

"Why?"

"My brother has been locked in a dungeon for sixteen years," he said. "He's not... If he has..."

"What are you saying? You think that your brother is a virgin as well?"

"It is entirely possible. And if not, then what manner of sexual contact has he had? Prostitutes? If they sent someone down to service him..."

"You don't really think that happened."

"I don't know. But I was counting on you having enough sexual experience that you would be able to... Ease the way between the two of you."

"Well, I don't. So if you're going to give lessons, Cairo, perhaps those are the lessons you should be giving."

The volley that was set out between them was... It was explosive. Dangerous. And she knew then and there that she had not been imagining the banked fire in his eyes. She knew that last night when she had wept with him holding on to her shoulders, she had not imagined the magnetic force between the two of them.

He wanted her. He wanted her. And that was the way of it.

He wanted her, and it was not imaginary. And she wanted him.

And she was supposed to marry his brother. She didn't want to.

And he wouldn't waver.

And then there was the fact that he was… He didn't seem to possess human feeling. Neither of them did, she was certain of that. For if Cairo spoke of Riyaz as being broken, then she could rest assured that he would be even more difficult.

And she'd wanted Cairo from the beginning.

His was the kiss she'd wanted all those years ago.

The one she hadn't been brave enough to claim.

"Do not say things like that."

"Why not?"

And yet again, she felt the wildness. The wildness pushing at her spirit. It was an accident but today she had dressed like Katherine Hepburn. Like she had a safari to go on. A lion to tame. She had known that she would need strength today.

And she had dressed accordingly. But she remembered the power she had felt, standing naked before the windows. With the wilderness in front of her. And she was suddenly seized by another urge.

You are insane. You've been kissed once. You don't have any experience.

That was true. But she had been right to run. It had gotten him to listen. Perhaps it had even gotten her some sympathy. So she would not question her instinct.

She began to unbutton her shirt. Slowly, purposefully, and she let it fall from her shoulders.

Then she unclasped her bra and let it fall as well.

She didn't dwell on the fact that he could see her. Rather she dwelled on how good it felt to have the air on her skin. The desert before her.

Cairo was the desert. She realized.

Cairo was the sand and the sky and the sun.

Cairo was Nazul. He always had been for her. And always would be. She unbuttoned her pants, unzipped them, kicked her shoes off as she pushed the pants and underwear down her legs.

And she was naked before him, as she had been before the desert.

But she understood now. That they were one in the same. Understood now, that this was why it felt right. That this was why it mattered.

And then she stood, completely naked and unashamed. "If you wish to teach me something of value. Teach me about pleasure."

CHAPTER TEN

IT WAS LIKE the whole world caved in on itself. Like the sound and the ever-loving fury had come to collect. In many ways, he was a man of discipline. And in many ways, a man of none. In many ways he was a man without equal, a man who would not be tested.

But the problem with Ariel was she had been trying him and testing him since he was a boy. The problem with Ariel was that she was symbolic of all that he hoped to achieve.

And the problem with Ariel was that she had just professed her innocence. And what would that mean? He was to give her beautiful virgin body over to his brother? A man who was little more than a beast?

To atone for his sins, he would compound them by giving her to Riyaz as if she was his to give, and maybe…

Maybe it would be better to let her choose him now. For this.

To be the first.

You know that isn't why you're bending here. It isn't for her. It's for you.

It didn't matter why. She didn't even know how to pleasure herself. And he… He was brought back to that moment when he had entered the jewel room. When he had shown her the crown. The necklace. The bracelets. He remembered the way that he had wanted to put them on her. The way he had wanted to take the silken scarf and wrap it around their hands.

As a boy, that had been the highest expression of his desire. As a boy, it had been his version of wishing to take her to bed, he supposed. He wanted to kiss her. That much she'd known.

And now here she was, naked before him. In her body was a glorious splendor that he had never seen before. The smooth cast of her skin. Pale pink nipples and high, firm breasts. The indent of her waist, the flare of her hips. But the shape was unimportant. It was that it was her. That was what mattered. That was what signified. It was what made her irresistible. It was what made her…

His.

He gritted his teeth together and curled his fingers into fists.

And he wondered... What she hoped to gain from this.

Riyaz never has to know.

No. He didn't. And he didn't know when he was going to be able to deliver her to Riyaz. But the beast within him hated those options. The beast within him roared against it. And yet he realized it would not be better. Not ever. The idea of any other man putting his hands on Ariel destroyed him.

But he had promised her to Riyaz. He had promised that he would fix this.

Fix this nation... He could not be what Ariel wanted or needed. And so the plan would have to remain in place.

But he could have her.

In the meantime, why could he not have her?

To teach her. To show her what her body could feel.

He refused to finish the thought. Refused to go down that road. For it was a fury within him.

She took a step toward him, and the crack of desire that went through him was like a bolt of lightning.

And if Riyaz had not requested her specifically, he would've abandoned the plan then.

Would have given her a chance to run. Either away from him or to him.

But Riyaz wanted her. Had asked for her by name, when he had spoken of nothing else from the past.

His brother seemed set on carrying out the plan as it had been laid out before them, so how could he deny him that?

But now...

He had taken this pause to ensure Ariel's safety.

He wished to ensure her safety in all things. He reached out his hand, brushed his fingertips along her cheek, and down, cupping her breasts and moving his thumb over her nipple. Her head fell back, her lips parting, a raw sound escaping her lips. "This is what you want?"

"Cairo..."

"You want to finish this thing that began to burn between us when we were children, is that it? Even knowing where it will end?"

"Cairo..."

"Why? Tell me your game. If this is simply a way that you think you can manipulate me... I cannot be manipulated, Ariel, and I will not be. I will not be taken in the way that my father was by yours. I will not yield. I owe my brother the life that he has missed, and he has demanded you. Thus, you will be given to him."

"But you're tempted," she said.

"Yes, I'm tempted. I'm tempted to show you all of the things that your body can do. Everything that it can feel. I am tempted to touch you until you're crying out my name. Until you are beneath me, with me buried inside of you. Yes, I am tempted. But to give in to the temptation will mean nothing. And you must understand that."

"I want a choice," she said. "It was always decided for me that Riyaz would be my husband. And it didn't matter that you were the one that I preferred."

Somewhere in all of that, he wanted to ask her. If she wanted the choice so badly why had she not made it when she was living life on her own? She could've been with anyone that she wanted to. She had not been. And he had to wonder why.

But the questions were lost in the feel of her soft skin beneath his palm. They were lost as lust clouded his vision. Overtook every reasonable thought. Made him more beast than man.

And here he was concerned that his brother would be too rough with her. Not have a care for her needs.

He found that he was on edge. Beside himself. Beyond himself.

He moved forward, one hand still on her breast, and with the other, cupped her chin. He stared at her for a long moment. Deep into those aqua eyes. And then he dipped his head and claimed her mouth.

He had wanted her, wanted this, since they were children, but he would not have known what to do with the electrical storm that it created.

It was almost too much for him now. A man of jaded tastes. A man who had taken more lovers than he could count.

Yes. He would have to see her in the palace, knowing that she could no longer be his. Knowing that she now gave her body to his brother. But the alternative was to see her, never having been inside of her.

She tasted of oranges. Strong coffee and a brightness that he had long since given up believing in. If he were honest, she tasted of his failure. But in the moment, it felt only like triumph. She felt like salvation. And much like when his plane had descended in these mountains, he wanted to roar. He was not in his brother's kingdom. Not now. He was in his own. In his element. And he was holding her in his arms. And she was his. He claimed her. Her soft naked body pressed up against his.

And the years were erased. Except he was a man now, and she was a woman. And he knew what he wanted of her.

"Let me show you," he said. "Let me show you what you can feel. Let me show you what your body can do." He put his hand between her legs and found her slick with wanting, and he continued to lick into her mouth, mirroring the exploration happening between her thighs. She was slick and eager, and he slid his thumb over the source of her pleasure, relishing her gasp of desire.

And he realized, as her pleasure coated his fingers, that everything had changed. That there was no question of her being given to his brother, or anyone. She was his. It did not matter what agreement his father had drawn up with hers. It did not matter what he owed Riyaz, what Riyaz wanted or what he'd asked for. She was his. She had been from the moment he had first seen her. No other man had ever touched her body, and no other man ever would.

She belonged to him. And if he had to wage a war...

To have her, that he would. To stake his claim on her body.

He pushed a finger inside of her and she made a small, sweet sound of desire.

He worked his finger in and out of her tight channel, need pulsing within him.

How he wanted her. How she belonged to him. He marveled at it.

Had it always been this? And had this always been fate? Had he ever really intended to get her for Riyaz, or had he always been intent on claiming her for himself?

Perhaps this was what he had been waiting for all along. His. His woman. It was his turn to take his place in the palace as well. He should also take a wife.

Intense possessiveness poured through him. "Mine," he said, the word hard. He added a second finger to the first, and her knees buckled. He tested her, teased her. And he could feel her entire body begin to tremble.

"Come for me," he growled.

He pressed his palm against the sensitized bundle of nerves at the apex of her thighs and she gasped, her knees buckling. And only he held her up.

"Cairo," she whispered.

"You are not a prisoner," he said, withdrawing his fingers from her body, rubbing his thumb over her lips. "You are my lover. You belong to me."

He picked her up off the ground and carried her out of the ballroom. She was stark naked. And she clung to him.

If any of the staff saw them, they quickly melted into the background, making themselves invisible. They would betray nothing. He knew that. He almost expected her to gasp with maidenly modesty at being paraded through the public space bare as she was. But she didn't. She only clung to him. And he was intent on making her his own.

Nothing else mattered. Nothing. He carried her up the stairs, and into his bedroom. One entire wall was a window that looked over the valley below.

The room felt exposed, though nobody could see up this far to see inside. And anyway, no one would ever be out in that unforgiving part of the desert. He set her down, on the highly polished floor, just in front of the window. He held her chin, guided her to look straight ahead. "Do you see? Down there, and ahead. That is Nazul. That is Riyaz's domain. But this here… This is mine. And while you are in it, you are mine as well. Do you remember when I showed you the jewels?"

"Yes. The jewels meant for Riyaz's bride."

"Yes. I showed them to you because I had a fantasy. Of putting them on your wrists.

Your head. Your neck. Of binding your hand to mine. I was but a fourteen-year-old boy. I knew nothing of life or the things which might happen in the future. I only knew that you belonged to Riyaz, and could not belong to me. But I wanted you to."

"I thought that you showed them to me to remind me. I didn't think…"

"Perhaps I was attempting to remind myself, but I do not think I was half so present. What I wanted, what I truly wanted, was to betray my brother."

And now… He had lived his life in service of freeing Riyaz. He would demand her payment. Yes. She would be his bride. His. He would bind her wrists with a red scarf before all the nation. And then he would bind her wrists with it in their room, his willing supplicant. Not a prisoner.

"From up here you are the queen of the desert," he said. "Look at the way the light shines on you. You have nothing to hide. You are beautiful. Glorious. Did you not take a lover because you did not know?"

She looked at him. "I didn't take a lover because I didn't care to. It is that simple."

"But I can feel your desire. The evidence of it still is coating my fingers."

She shivered. "Perhaps it is because I left

my desire with you. It is a scary thought. That you hold the key to my desire. I did not wish that it were true. When we knew one another we were innocent. At least, it felt innocent to me."

"It was," he said. "I was drawn to you. I thought you were beautiful. But I did not think of stripping you naked. I thought of kissing your lips. I thought of marrying you, but not of taking you to bed. And now... I am consumed by the idea of thrusting inside of you. Deep and hard. Feeling your tight wet body closed around mine. Would you like that? My possession?"

"Yes," she whispered.

"You understand that there will be no question of you going to Riyaz after this?"

She looked wide-eyed and confused. "There won't be?"

"No. You will be giving up the throne in exchange for the knowledge of my body. Does that seem a fair trade to you?"

His body ached. Pulsed with desire. He needed her to say yes. He needed it more than he needed his next breath.

"Yes," she said.

"There is no turning back from this. There will be no remaking the moment into something else. We are not children trading oranges in a garden."

"I understand."

He wondered if she did. But he was past the point of talking. He took her hand and pinned it to her lower back, walked her up toward the window, sweeping her hair to the side and exposing her neck. Then he pinned her other hand with the first, holding her fast with one hand wrapped around both of her wrists. He kissed her neck, and she arched forward, her breasts pressing against the window. He grunted in approval. This game of both possessing her and making a show of displaying her appealed to something darkly possessive within him.

He himself was not a modest man. He had never thought much of engaging in intimacy and semi-public places if the opportunity presented itself. But he could not say that he had ever taken particular pleasure in it either. But there was something about this moment. The declaration of it. The pleasure deferred that made it feel like a rush. A flood of excitement that overtook everything.

"Imagine, if the sands below were filled with adoring subjects. Watching how I worship you. Gazing upon your beauty."

He heard the sound of her swallowing hard in the silence of the room.

"It excites you."

"I don't know why."

"Because you like that I make you like this. Only me. Is that true? Do you wish the world to know that only I make you so wet? That only I could ever entice you to such sin?"

"You arouse me, it's true. But I like to think that I'm wild enough to stand naked before the desert all on my own. Aren't I the one who asked for this?"

"It's true you did. You are a wild woman in your soul. And I find that it is a beautiful thing."

She would not have made a sheikha. She was too... Untamed. She was not what Riyaz needed. But for him... For Cairo she would be perfect.

He pulled her away from the window, turned her so that she was facing him, and still keeping her wrists captive, brought her against his body, claimed her mouth in a deep, hard kiss. "You're beautiful," he said. "And mine."

"You said that," she whispered.

"And I will keep saying it. Until it is a tattoo on your soul. Until you know it as well as you know it is time to draw a breath lest you perish. You were always mine, Ariel."

And it was good that he was doing this. Because the alternative would be to betray his brother once he had already taken her as his wife. Cairo knew his limitations, and Ariel Hart was the hardest of those limitations. She was the one thing he could not resist. The one thing he could not endure.

And he would've had her. "Was that your first orgasm?" he asked, his mouth close to hers.

Her cheeks turned pink, and she nodded slowly.

"Did you like it?"

"It makes me want things. Wild things. Things I never would've thought I could want."

"Yes. That is the problem with pleasure. It can turn us into strangers to ourselves. Can make something that would not sound appealing at all the most enticing thing on earth. I wish to feast upon you. Lay you open on that bed for me and lick you until you scream my name."

Interest sparked in the depths of her eyes, and she shivered. "What are you waiting for, then?"

He growled and lifted her up, setting her

down on the center of the bed and forcing her knees apart. He looked down at her, the flushed, swollen heart of her, slick with her desire for him. "Tell me who is about to plea-sure you, Ariel."

"Cairo," she said.

"I gave you an orange in the garden to show you the pleasures of my country. And now I will feast upon you like you're ripened fruit, to show you the pleasures of your own body. I will give you everything good. I take care of what is mine." He pressed his thumb against the pearl between her swollen lips and rubbed it slowly across that sensitized flesh. She moaned and shook, and he slid his thumb down and penetrated her slowly. Then he leaned forward, kissing her inner thigh be-fore sucking the source of her pleasure into his mouth until she cried out. He licked her, savoring the flavor of her as he moved his fingers in and out of her body.

"Cairo," she said, her voice trembling.

"Yes," he growled. He did not feel like a civilized man. He was the barbarian warrior of his people's past. And he had claimed a woman. She was his war prize. Not Riyaz's. She was his. He had claimed her. He was the one that had righted the wrongs that had been done against their family. It was not Riyaz's fault that he had been a prisoner. That his hands had been bound and he had not been able to claim revenge. But Cairo had done so. He had deposed the imposters. The woman should be his.

And he would claim that honor before his brother. He vowed it.

He licked and sucked, rubbing two fingers within her slick channel until she found her release again. And then again.

Until she was begging him to stop. Even as she clung to his shoulders to keep him from moving away.

She was becoming ready for his possession. And the idea of it caused his masculinity to harden painfully.

He moved up her body, kissing her stomach, sucking her nipple deep within his mouth. She had the most perfect body. Because it was hers.

"Are you ready for me?"

He was still fully clothed. And he moved away from her, taking his shirt off slowly. He watched as her eyes widened, as hunger darkened them.

When he removed the rest of his clothing, he saw a bit of fear there. He was not a small man. It was true. But her fear turned to hunger after only a moment. She sat up, moving to the edge of the bed. She kissed his stomach, down to his Adonis belt and to the sensitized crown of his arousal, where she ran her tongue around the head of him before taking him inside of her mouth. He growled, gripping her hair with his hand. And pushed himself deeper into the welcoming heat of her mouth. He should have a care because of her innocence, he thought at first. But then... She should know. She should know what sort of man she was allowing into her bed. There was something to be said for starting as you meant to go on. And now that she was his...

Theirs was not a gentle desire. Why pretend that it was?

He rocked his hips forward and back, and she took him as deep as she could, swirling her tongue around his length as she did.

When he was close, too close, he moved away from her. He put his hand between her legs and found her slippery for him still, and he kissed her mouth, moving her back onto the bed as he positioned himself between her thighs. He pressed himself to the entrance of her body and entered her slowly. She closed her eyes, arching her back up off the bed as he moved into her, inch by agonizing inch.

He growled as he thrust fully home, and she gripped his shoulders hard, digging her fingernails into his flesh. He took the pain as his due, as he was certain the breaching of her maidenhead had caused her pain as well.

This should hurt. It was right that it be painful. They had waited so long. It should be everything.

He might have taken his share of lovers, but he had never had Ariel. And that made it new. Singular. Set apart from every other experience. And every other person.

He had given himself over to a life of hedonistic pleasure, something, anything to drown out the pain of what he had lost. The only way that he had been able to function for a great number of years was to blot everything out. Drink. Sex. Oblivion was the name of the game.

But this was not oblivion. Here, he was present. Here, it was sharp. Real. The feeling of being inside of her was not like anything else.

And he began to move. And he watched as the slight discomfort on her face transformed. Bloomed into wonder. And he felt that same bloom echo inside of himself. They were both of them brilliant. Made new in this storm of desire.

She wrapped her legs around his waist, a raw cry shattering the silence of the room.

And she hadn't even come yet. Each thrust made her whimper. And he found himself growling in response. And then he felt it. The ripples of her next release. The promise of her completion. Then he let himself go. He held her hips as he drove into her, hard, ruthless. And when she screamed with pleasure, he allowed himself that same rush.

But it was not a blur. Not a blessed moment of nothing as it often was. Instead, it was her. Ariel. Everything.

A heightened sense of his partner, rather than an isolated moment of release.

Even his own pleasure was somehow about her. And that was a revelation.

She looked up at him, soft with a small smile on her lips. "Well, if I would've known that it was like that I might not have waited so long."

"Believe me," he said, his voice rough. "That was singular."

"Good."

"There is no question about you marrying Riyaz now…you know that."

"You said. And I… I decided. But I don't know what it means."

"We are still going back to Nazul. But instead of marrying him… You will marry me."

CHAPTER ELEVEN

SHE FELT LIKE she was in a state of shock. She had just lost her virginity and quite spectacularly to the man that had haunted her dreams and fantasies for the better part of her life.

And now he was… Now he was telling her that she was going to marry him. And not his brother.

But nowhere in any of this had she ever been given a choice. Not about anything.

He gave you a choice. He told you. You were choosing to not be with Riyaz.

Still. It was a limited set of options.

And yet…

She couldn't imagine leaving Cairo. Not after that.

But when it came right down to it she didn't know him.

And the fact that she had feelings for him made all of this feel much more fraught. She didn't care for Riyaz. Had never kissed him or made love to him. Marrying him had felt like something hollow she could not wrap her mind around. But it hadn't felt… Like it might shatter her,

That was the thing. She had no feelings for Riyaz. She had far too many for Cairo.

She didn't know what she wanted. She couldn't imagine going back to Paris and acting as if this had never happened. It wasn't even her goal. Not anymore. But she also couldn't… She couldn't fathom… She couldn't imagine how they had gone from him being so set on handing her over to Riyaz to this.

"Surely you must have known the moment I put my hands on you that you were mine? It was foolish of us to deny it. This has been… I see it now," he said. "I see it now with clarity. This has been inevitable. You and I have always been on this path. Perhaps I survived to find you."

The words were almost romantic, except they sounded tortured. Torn from him as if by force.

"Cairo… I don't understand. You've never made any indication that you wish to marry anyone in…"

"I will marry you. For it must be decisive. And I must claim you. You must be mine.

There is no opening for Riyaz to have you then."

"And what will you do?"

"I will marry you before taking you to the palace. We had our wedding feast after all. And our wedding night."

"How will you do that?"

"I will get a preacher to come and marry us, obviously. Clergy are not so hard to come by. I will have one flown in."

"Why?"

"There's nothing he can do."

"I thought that him being the sheikh meant that he could do anything he wanted."

"Perhaps. But I believe that he will respect it. He will respect that I have claimed you in this way. It is something he can understand."

"You speak of him like he's an animal."

"Not an animal. But a warrior. He has spent these long years turning himself into a weapon. But so have I."

"Cairo... What of love? Of children?"

"I did not use protection when I took you. Children may be an inevitability of the passion that we find between ourselves. Love has nothing to do with marriage." He looked at her, his black eyes dark. "Passion has nothing to do with love. Fate is not love, is it?"

"I don't know," she said. "But I..."

"And what love have you seen in your life? Did your father love you? Did he love your mother?"

"I don't know. I don't know. I haven't seen it."

"Do not worry about love. Think of what I can make you feel."

"And my career?"

It didn't actually seem that important in the moment.

"You may have whatever you wish. My moon, I will not keep you prisoner."

"But you won't let me go either."

He shook his head. "No. I will not."

"That is being a prisoner, Cairo. Just one with privileges."

"Then I will be your jailer as well as your husband. I had hoped that you might decide for yourself that you wished to stay."

She wasn't sure she wanted to leave. That was for certain. But just for a moment... Just for a moment she imagined what it might have been like if the two of them would have met on a busy city street. If he would have asked her to dinner, and she would've said yes. If they would've gone to the movies and eaten popcorn. And he would've kissed her good-night on the doorstep, and she would have done something wild like have sex with him that first date, and felt just slightly guilty but not regretful. And made a promise to see him again. And again and again. She wasn't sure that she wanted to leave him. But she wasn't sure how she felt about him issuing life sentences. And she just wished…

She just wished that she might have been a different woman. And him a different man. She just wished that it might've been… Fate that had brought them together in a different way. And not this hard and sharp reality. Not Stockholm syndrome.

Maybe it had always been Stockholm syndrome.

"I will have someone here to wed us by nightfall."

"Cairo…"

"I will not leave any room for this to fall apart. I will not leave any room for him to take you from me. That is all."

And this was her life, she realized. Being caught between two impossible alpha males. This man, who sought to bend the world to his sheer will in spite of the fact that he was not—by birth order—the heir to the throne of his country.

And his older brother who was.

And she didn't know why in the world both of them were so hell-bent on having her.

She wondered if any of it was actually about her. Even for Cairo. And he always just wanted what his brother had? Had it always simply been about… Being denied something that he wanted because of birth order? She knew that he wanted her. Physically. It was apparent. The passion between them had been intense, and even if she did not have experience, she knew that it was real. And extremely hot. She knew that.

But that didn't mean that it wasn't spurred on by something else. A more complicated emotion than even he realized.

He would tell her that he didn't have emotions. And she knew that he had been through more than she could understand. She knew that while she had been hurt by what had happened to his family, it wasn't the same.

She did know that.

At least, she hoped she did. She hoped that he was choosing this, as she had chosen him.

"I must go see to some business."

"I see." He kissed her. Rough and hard, it tethered her to the moment. Tethered her to the earth. He wanted her. Whatever else existed beneath the surface, he wanted her. That was… It was something. It was something good to know anyway.

"You see. All will be well."

The hours passed slowly. The first thing that arrived was not a clergyman, but a gown. White and lace. And definitely not something traditional. It was long-sleeved, with a high neck, but the lace was see-through. The petals of the flowers would just cover her nipples, but only just, and her skin would show through the fabric. The woman who had done her hair and makeup the first day she had been in residence appeared. "Cairo has requested that I see to your preparations for the wedding."

"Do you not find that strange?"

The woman ducked her head. "No. I've seen the way he looks at you. Since he first brought you here. I know that he intended for you to marry the sheikh. But I could see that he had passion for you. You are very lucky. He is a wonderful man."

The way the woman said it was tinged with jealousy, and even though it wasn't a pointed or mean jealousy, it made Ariel feel just a little bit guilty. They had upended a whole lot of things.

She styled Ariel's hair expertly, and did her makeup so that she looked fresh-faced and glowing. As for the dress… The only thing she was given to wear underneath it was a white thong, which made the entire thing seem rather like extremely fancy lingerie.

Everything was covered. But only just.

She had a feeling that her groom would not be in anything quite so scandalous.

But just the thought of him in a dark suit cut around the lines of his body made her mouth go dry.

In fairness, what women found sexy was slightly different than what men found sexy. She didn't wish to see him in see-through mesh.

Her lips twitched, and so did her body, in such a way that she thought maybe she wouldn't mind it. But then, she didn't mind the look of Cairo altogether.

The moment of levity was welcome. Because otherwise she just felt... Blindsided. By everything that had happened.

And yet at the same time it felt... Like that thread had been tied back together. There was a great knot at the middle, and you couldn't untangle it without undoing the bond. It wasn't seamless. And it spoke to the fact that there had been a number of years between this moment and the last when they had been together.

But still... It did feel like a continuation of

something. Like a piece of herself had been restored, that had before been lost.

Maybe she did have to accept the fact that Cairo was her fate.

"He is outside," said Aisha after Ariel went downstairs.

"Will you... Will you let me outside?"

"You can do that yourself," the other woman said, smiling.

Ariel walked slowly to the door and extended her hand. And it gave way to her.

Her heart expanded in her chest. That was a sign of something. Of trust. A prisoner with privileges.

She tried to tamp down her reaction to it.

She walked outside into the heat, the sun painting the sky pink as it began to set on the horizon. And there was Cairo. Standing there with a man in robes. And there was a horse beside him, with a garland around his neck. As if he too had been dressed for the wedding. He looked at her, his gaze filled with heat, and she couldn't help but be swept away in the moment.

"My moon," he said. "Give me your hands."

She did so. And the officiant handed him two cuffs. He put them on her wrists. Then the officiant handed him the necklace, and he fastened it around her neck.

And what he took out next was not a crown, but a simple circle of gems, with a teardrop ruby at the center. And slowly, very carefully, he pinned it to her hair, the gem resting at the center of her forehead. Where he had touched her with his thumb that day in the ballroom.

"And now we can begin," he said.

The officiant then took the red silk scarf and bound their hands together. But this was not a rehearsal. This was real. They were real.

"With your mind. With your mouth. With your heart. Obey me." She found herself nodding as he made the commandments, as he touched her with his thumb. And then she returned the proclamation. "With your thoughts. With your words. With your heart."

"And though we now remove the scarf," the officiant said. "The words have bonded you. Hold hands through life, but remember, even when you let go, these promises are meant to keep you, bound to one another. Bound to your union, to your commitment. There is nothing that can undo a spiritual bond such as this one. You are husband and wife. And there is none but death that can separate you. And even then, your souls will find one another amongst the stars."

And he released the scarf from around their

hands. But she could still feel it there. And they held on to each other still.

"Thank you," Cairo said. "I trust you will file all necessary paperwork upon your return?"

"Yes. Though I will have it sent to no school until your brother's fire cools. And I will remain in Turkey until that point."

"I do not blame you. Thank you again."

And then suddenly she found herself being swept up onto the back of a horse. She gasped as Cairo lifted her from the ground and set her in front of him. And with a decisive, masculine command, he spurred the horse into a gallop. And on they went. He held on to her, his arm around her waist as they tore through the desert sand, a cloud of earth billowing behind them. She couldn't have asked him what they were doing if she wanted to. He wouldn't have been able to hear her over the sound of the hoofbeats, and she wouldn't have been able to shout it into the rushing wind.

They rode across the sands, away from the house, away from everything. And the farther and farther they got from everyone else, the more it felt… Right. The less she felt a prisoner. And then she saw it, in the distance, just as the sun dipped entirely behind the mountain and blanketed the earth in darkness.

There was a stake and a feeding trough set out there for the horse, and a bonfire lit there as well. There was a spread of food next to it. And she had a feeling that whoever had set it up must have just vacated, as it might otherwise have been a target for animals.

"And here is where we will spend our wedding night," he said, bringing the horse to a stop.

But it was the tent that caught her focus. Large and elaborate, with brightly colored tapestries all along the outside.

She could feel his heart raging behind her, and her own beats in a fiery response.

"Why?" It was the only thing she could think to say. And she wasn't sure why it mattered. But she was curious. Why not go to the sumptuously appointed rooms back there?

"Because the desert has always called to us, has it not?"

Her heart surged in rebuttal of that statement. "I used to hate it here."

"No. You didn't. You hated feeling bound in the face of such wildness. But you are not. Not with me. Here we are free."

He helped her off the horse, and then took their steed and tied him to the wooden post outside. Then he took her hand and led her inside the tent. The tent was one large room with a star shape on the roof, and a hanging lantern made of fractured glass at the center. There was a large, sumptuously appointed bed at the center of it. Scarves hanging around the frame. It was entirely there for sex. And she had a feeling so was Cairo. The dress that he had chosen for her certainly suggested that. "There is an oasis just past the tent. There may be animals at it, but they will not bother us."

"Why do you think that? Because you're with me?"

"Yes. And they would not dare." He began to take his clothing off, slowly, and she watched him, rapt. He took his white shirt off first, exposing acres of bronzed muscle. His abdominal muscles shifted as he began to undo his belt, as he took his shoes off and everything else, leaving him completely naked to her gaze. And aroused. He was glorious. A warrior made into sensual reality right before her. His arousal was strong and thick, his thighs well-muscled. And everything feminine within her reacted to the sight of him.

"Take off your dress. And then we will walk to the oasis."

"What?"

"You have wanted to walk naked in the

desert this entire time. You want to be like this in the open. It excites you."

And she felt ashamed just then. Only slightly. But why? Why should she? She had never known what to do with her sexuality, because it had never felt like it was entirely her own. She had been put in a situation where she was meant to give herself to a man she hadn't chosen. And when she did meet a man she actually cared for... He was forbidden to her. And then she had thought he was gone and...

It just wasn't easy. Any of this. It was terrifying and exciting all at once.

And the truth was, even if Cairo had given her limited options, when it came to wanting him, there was no doubt about the fact that she did.

She wanted him. That was simply the truth of it. There was no coercion when it came to her desire for him.

And maybe... Maybe he was right. Maybe this was what she wanted. Maybe she wanted it so badly because she had never felt like her sexuality, her body was her own. But that was the strange and amazing gift of wanting Cairo. It was a rebellion. And... By wanting her in return, he had also rebelled. It was a heady realization indeed. He had wanted nothing more than to serve Riyaz, than to give him what he wanted, but he had rebelled entirely by doing this. And with that truth, she could see her own power.

Clearly. Absolutely.

So she began to slowly take her gown off, revealing her bare curves beneath, the brief pair of underwear, which she took off quickly. She had never been ashamed to be naked in front of him.

"Come," he said, taking her hand and leading her out of the tent.

The night air kissed her skin, and her heart began to beat faster, as she thought of that trip into the desert when they had been young.

He looked at her, the smile on his face almost boyish, and it made her wonder if he was thinking of the same thing. They walked slowly, even though the ground was soft.

"If when we were teenagers... If I had kissed you..."

"It frightens me to think of what might've happened," he said. "We would've been too young for such an explosion of passion, don't you think?"

"I do," she said. "And yet I'm not sure that would have stopped either of us."

"I'm not sure we would have known how to stop."

"We're both nearly thirty, Cairo. And we did not stop when we touched. We definitely wouldn't have had the maturity to do it then."

"True." He tightened his hold on her hand. "But you are my wife now. And we can do whatever we please. You are no longer forbidden to me."

The words were dark and delicious. They made her shiver.

They came over a small hill, and that was when she could see the pool of water. Two jackals out on the edge looked up when they approached. But the little dogs scampered off into the distance as they approached.

"I told you they would not make nuisances of themselves. They have no real desire to interact with a person, at least not unless we are in much worse shape. They prefer an easier fight." He held his hand out to her. "Come. Into the water."

The water was warm from the sun, just perfect, and she took his hand and allowed him to lead her into it.

He wrapped his arm around her waist, and dragged her deeper, held her as they floated, chest to chest, the sound of the waves lapping against their skin calming and arousing at once. "And I would have you beneath the light of the moon," he said.

"And I would let you."

Right now they felt like younger versions of themselves. Less complicated versions of themselves. Without murder and kidnappings and betrayal between them. But perhaps this was the truth of them. As they might have been without such complications.

And for tonight, she would revel in it.

"When a warrior took a bride, he would bring her out into the desert to consummate. So that the entire tribe would not hear the sounds of their pleasure. Of course, a hazard of living in tents is that you often did hear the lovemaking of others. But that first night... Warriors and kings were able to keep the cries of their women to themselves. That is why I brought you out here."

"I don't care if anyone hears."

"I know you don't. And neither do I. But still... It seemed right."

It did. She didn't need any further explanation. It just did. He stood them both up, and he began to move his hands smoothly over her water slick skin. She sighed, as he moved his hands up to cup her breasts, to tease her nipples. "You are a goddess. A temptress. And I ought to love you for it. But I cannot. I ought to love myself, and I cannot. For I have one. I have one you." She knew that she should object to that. To such masculine, possessive language. And yet she found she couldn't. And she gave up trying by the time one hand moved around to cup her rear, then moved deeper, delving between her thighs, teasing her. Penetrating her. She gave up all resistance after that. And she simply surrendered.

He lowered his head and suckled her nipple between his lips, drawing her in deep as he continued to tease her with his finger.

She rocked her hips against him, found the blunt head of his arousal, used it to soothe that sensitized bundle of nerves between her legs.

She rocked her hips as he pushed two fingers within her, and her orgasm unraveled within her. She gasped, calling out his name.

And then he swallowed her cries with a deep kiss.

She collapsed against him, and he lifted her up out of the water, carrying her back to shore. All the way back to the tent.

The bonfire yet raged, and there was food there for them still. But there was also a blanket spread out in the sand, and he laid her down upon it. Water dripped from her breasts, sliding down slowly, the cool sensations making her long for the touch of his hands. Then again, anything would make her long for the touch of his hands.

She was bare, open to the sky, and just the thought of it made her internal muscles pulse. And then there he was, above her, every inch the hardened warrior. He knelt down beside her, kissed her mouth, her neck, down to her breast again, down her stomach, until he found himself between her legs. He seemed to enjoy doing that. Seemed to enjoy the taste of her, and she loved the way that he licked her deep.

She rocked her hips restlessly in time with the wicked pass of his tongue, his teeth, the deep, rough penetration of his fingers. Two, and then three, which made her gasped. She rolled her hips along with him, begging, pleading his name toward the sky as if it were a prayer.

When her orgasm hit, it hit hard. Her internal muscles clenching around his finger as she cried out.

He removed them, and then slid them into his own mouth, licking them clean, a little ripple of need making her whimper as he did so, his dark eyes never breaking contact with hers. He lay down on the blanket beside her, then gripped her hips, and settled her over him, guiding her slowly onto the blunt head of his erection. And she took him in, inch by inch. "You are free. Ride me."

She let her head fall back as she began to let her hips rock, as she moved up and down, setting a torturous rhythm that both pleased and tormented them both.

Out there in the open air, she cupped her own breast, toying with her nipple as she moved over him, allowing him to watch her as she tightened her own pleasure.

"Put your other hand between your legs," he said roughly. She did so, rubbing at the source of her desire there before stroking her fingers along either side of where he penetrated her. Making them both cry out.

She didn't have experience. But she wanted him. And she had no shame in that desire. And it was the lack of shame that made everything feel brilliant. That made it all feel wonderful. That made everything she did seem right and make sense.

Suddenly, he growled, reversing their positions so that he was over her. And she gloried in that. And the dominance of it. She had enjoyed where she sat, so she could take him in and give him a show as well. But she loved his weight over her, the strong heat of that steel within her. The way his eyes blazed down into hers. And then he began to move, each thrust within her hard and fast taking her breath away.

Oh, how she needed this. Needed him.

And suddenly, pleasure began to ripple within her. And she climaxed before she even knew that it was building, her shocked scream of pleasure echoing around them. And he followed closely behind, lowering his head and growling like the most ferocious beast of the desert. She felt him pulse within her, felt him spill his seed deep.

And she rocked her hips in time with the pulsing of his release, wringing out every last bit of pleasure between the two of them.

And then they lay there. Naked and unashamed beneath the night sky.

"I told you you would like the desert at night," he said, his voice rough. "It only took me sixteen years to show you why."

"And I have wondered about that old unfulfilled promise so many nights since," she whispered.

She dragged her fingers over his chest, luxuriating in the muscle, the heat, the crisp hair.

All the textures of who he was.

"Come, my bride," he said. "You must be hungry."

They sat naked in front of the fire and ate their wedding meal. Different than the one they had had the other night. This one was much more rustic, but no less delicious. And she was ravenous.

Then he doused the fire and took her inside, made love to her over and over again in the big bed, until the sounds of morning began to be heard through the canvas walls.

And then she clung to him and slept. And she knew, as she drifted off to sleep, that she had made her choice.

She was no longer a prisoner. She chose him.

CHAPTER TWELVE

HE THOUGHT HE was dreaming. But there was a sound. Persistent and rhythmic, and it did not stop. In fact, it only seemed to be getting closer. And closer. And then the walls of the tent began to move. A mighty wind flexing them inward. He sat up. Ariel was pressed to his side, naked, her bare bottom scooted as hard up against his morning erection as possible.

And even in spite of the fact that there was something happening, what he found he wanted to do was roll her over onto her back and claim her. But he could not. Because...

Suddenly, the last vestiges of sleep and sexual drugging faded.

It was a helicopter.

It was his brother.

"Dress," he said quickly. He put on a pair of pants, and Ariel began to silently scramble behind him, putting the white wedding dress back on that she discarded the night before. It revealed too much of her body, but nothing could be done about that.

He heard the moment the helicopter landed.

He could hear a woman's voice. Sharp and persistent.

Brianna.

And then the tent flap opened, and a dark figure blotted out the sun.

Riyaz.

His dark hair was shoulder-length, he'd refused to cut it. His frame massive and uncompromising. He had scars on his face that twisted his formerly easy good looks into something much more challenging to behold.

And just behind him was Brianna. Her red hair scooped up into a ponytail, her eyes wide.

"And here I find you. With mine," said Riyaz.

"My apologies," said Cairo. "She is no longer yours. I have married her. And we have consummated it. Quite thoroughly, you will find."

"So I see." He looked around the tent, his gaze assessing. And it was impossible to tell what Riyaz thought about anything. It always had been. But he was yet more inscrutable after all his years of being locked away. Brianna touched his arm, and he saw his brother's entire body react. It went stiff, and then… calm. "What is it?" he asked, looking at her.

"You don't want to kill your brother," she said.

He took her chin in his hand. "I know that, *habibti*. I don't intend to." Then he turned back to Cairo, and there was no softness remaining. "The dungeon might be suitable."

"The dungeon. Is that what you think? And will you throw Ariel there as well?"

"I am the sheikh. I could marry her if I choose, regardless of whether or not she is bound to you." It was the most words he had ever heard Riyaz use in a sentence since coming out of the dungeon. It seemed as if Brianna's work with him had been quite accomplished.

"Or I could throw her in there with you. Or… Take two wives."

"Two wives."

"Yes," he said. "For I have already decided who I will marry."

"You said that you wanted to marry her," Cairo said, gesturing to Ariel.

"I said for you to bring her to me. I said it was what I required. I did not say why. I had thought that I might marry her. But I have decided on another course of action."

"What is that?"

"I'm marrying Brianna."

Brianna's eyes went round.

"Riyaz…"

"It will be no argument," he said. "You are mine. Or have I not made you so these last days?" Brianna's face turned red. And it did not take a great detective to figure out exactly what had been going on between his good friend and his brother.

"The situation is complicated, I see," Cairo said. "How dare you burst into my wedding tent given that you already decided what you plan to do?"

"I have not said yes," said Brianna. "I'm not yours. I don't live here. I'm not a citizen of this country. I don't…"

"You're mine now," he said. "Our bodies do not lie. You have lain with me, and you will be my wife."

Brianna was getting redder and redder. "Can you please not announce…?"

"You have stormed into the aftermath of my wedding night," Cairo said to Brianna. "Why should you be embarrassed to have your own activities commented upon?"

"Cairo," she said. "I'm sorry I…"

"You know, both of you could ask the women around you what they want," Ariel said. "Just because a woman sleeps with you it does not mean she wishes to marry you. Just because she is born doesn't mean she wishes to marry you. Just because her father says."

"Yes," said Brianna. "Exactly that."

"It is done," said Cairo. "You are my wife."

"I'm not his wife," said Brianna.

Riyaz looked her up and down. "You will be. Soon. Perhaps we might find someone out here to do the deed."

"You cannot get married in a desert," said Cairo. "You must have a wedding that is symbolic for the people."

"You do not get to order me around. I have spent enough time in captivity."

"But are not concerned at all about putting others in captivity," said Ariel. "I'm pleased that you're alive, Riyaz," she said. "But it doesn't give you license to act like a monster."

"Monster or not. You're both coming with me. Back to Nazul. These games have gone on long enough. It is time I begin my rule."

And that was how Ariel found herself bundled up in her see-through wedding dress and put into a helicopter. She could scarcely fathom what was happening to her. And she didn't think that the other woman had any idea of what was happening either.

The helicopter ride was short, as Cairo had said it would be. She thought of all the clothing she had left behind at the house in no man's land. Another life that she had to leave behind because of the dictates of these men.

She looked at Brianna—she thought that was the other girl's name—and the other woman looked back with a strange sort of wide-eyed misery.

She wondered what sort of life Brianna had left behind to be here. What sort of life she had not intended to leave.

The helicopter touched down in front of the palace. Golden and bright as she remembered it. It was strange how much the same it looked. It didn't seem like it should be possible. It had been polluted. Perverted by the violence and death of the royal family. By the fact that Riyaz had spent years living in the dungeon. And yet it had the audacity to look the same. They got out of the helicopter. And suddenly, there were servants ushering them into the palace.

"I must speak to my brother," said Cairo. "Brianna, please stay with Ariel."

Brianna looked mutinous, but then the two men left, and Ariel and Brianna were ushered into a plush sitting room. There were drinks sitting there. Something that looked like lemon with mint in it. She thought of resisting it, but then also thought that it might be a bit spiteful for no real reason. So she poured herself a measure of liquid.

"I take it you didn't expect to get a proposal."

Brianna's eyebrows shot up. "Was it a proposal? I thought it was a command."

"I think in their world that passes as a proposal. At least in my experience."

"They seem to think that getting naked with them means a proposal."

Ariel laughed. "Well. Yes."

"I loved him, you know."

She looked at her. "Riyaz?"

Brianna shook her head. "Never mind. Never mind. It's all very complicated now. And…"

Cairo. Brianna meant Cairo. Because of course they knew each other. That was the woman that he had spoken of that he had saved. The one he had talked to on the phone.

Ariel felt both guilty, and possessive in the moment.

But Cairo was her husband, so there was no reason to go being territorial about it. Especially not when Riyaz had already made proclamations about the fact that they were to get married. Unless…

"Cairo said that he was very… He's dangerous. He didn't hurt you? He didn't force you…"

The redhead's face went a scalding shade of strawberry. "He didn't force me to do anything. I was… A willing participant. He is… Complicated. And I somehow managed to get swept up in the complication."

That undersold the situation.

"And what are we to do?"

"I don't know."

CHAPTER THIRTEEN

CAIRO FACED HIS BROTHER, who sat on the throne, looking ill-suited to the position. Their father had been sophisticated. Always well-dressed. Always well-groomed. Riyaz looked like a relic from another time. And a rather dangerous one at that.

"Are you going to kill me?"

"No. Enough blood has been shed in these halls. I am deeply uninterested in killing you over a woman that I do not want. I want Brianna."

"Does Brianna want you?"

"She seems to want me well enough when she is naked with me."

Cairo did not especially wish to think of his friend that way. Or his brother.

"She did not seem particularly like she wishes to marry you, though."

He waved his hand. "Neither did Ariel. Did she wish to marry you?"

"That's different."

"Why? Because Brianna is your friend, and you feel possessive of her?"

"Did you only decide to have her to get at me? Was she collateral?"

"Do you love her?"

"No," said Cairo. "Not like you mean."

"She loves you."

Riyaz looked… Mystified by that. Haunted by it.

Guilt stabbed his chest. "She doesn't really. She idolizes me because I rescued her. It is not the same."

"It is. She would've chosen you. Though… She cannot resist me. These are inconvenient things. Bodies. I have had no prior experience with it. It is… Intoxicating."

Yet again more information than Cairo had wanted about his brother and his friend. "Marry her then," he said. "But you must have a ceremony that gives the country hope. And you cannot have a bride that looks as though she is being forced."

"I will handle it. And there will be no consequence for you and Ariel. It is also a good thing, I think," he said slowly. "Yes. It is a good thing. Her marrying you or me… The end result is the same. It puts to right something that was wrong. It does not allow her father to have the final say, and it… It may heal something. For our people."

"You are not quite so far gone as you allowed me to believe."

"I was," he said. "Brianna is remarkable."

Brianna might not love Riyaz, but he had the feeling that Riyaz loved Brianna. Whether or not his brother would openly apply that word to it or not. "We will announce your marriage, and my upcoming nuptials before the people. I will appear before them for the first time." He nodded. "Yes. This is the way. It will be an excellent first appearance."

"You should get a haircut," said Cairo.

"No. There are certain things about my experience that I cannot erase," he said, gesturing to the scars on his face. "And there are certain things that I choose to keep. I will never be the king that our father was. After what I've been through, it's impossible. But I will work to win back every single year that I lost. Every single year we all lost. I will be the ruler this country needs. On that you can trust me. Now. There are apartments set aside for you and your wife. Apartments fitting the new head of the military. We all have our responsibilities."

Ariel was still sitting in the room with Brianna when Cairo appeared. "Good news. We're not being thrown in the dungeon."

"That is good news," she said softly.

He extended his hand. "There are apartments set aside for us. And I have been given a new position. I'm to be head of the military. And we are to be presented as husband and wife tomorrow before the nation. It is when it will be announced that we have reclaimed the country."

Her heart kicked into gear. "You mean… Everyone will know. That you're back? That he's back?"

"Yes." It was scary, actually. Knowing that it would create a political shift in the world to have their identities revealed. Knowing that it would change… Everything.

And she and Cairo were simply… Married. They were married. It was something she could not yet wrap her mind around.

He nodded at Brianna, and then took Ariel's hand and led her from the room. "She's afraid," said Ariel. "Just because she slept with Riyaz does not mean that she wants to marry him."

"I'm sorry. I think these are the consequences for her actions and she has to deal with them."

"She's your friend."

"I know. And if… If I feel like Riyaz is being unreasonable, I will intervene. But I actually think he cares for her. He will not hurt her."

"Cairo," she said slowly. "I'm only going to ask you this once. Are you… Giving your friend to your brother because you feel guilty about what we did?"

"It isn't guilt. But I will not oppose what my brother wants. I understand that you wish… You wish for me to be more civilized. I lived in your world for all this time, after all. I understand that you wish to believe that our marriage indicates that I am something that I am not. The truth is, I am from this land. I am the second son of the royal family. And my duty is to my brother. My king. My duty is to the people here. I do not have a concern for anyone's feelings. Brianna will not be harmed. She will be sheikha. She will be well treated. I have no need to intervene."

"She said she doesn't want to stay."

"It is a shame. But always was a possibility…"

"You said you rescued her. You said you

rescued her and now you're willing to sacrifice her for this? What was the point of rescuing her at all?"

"Believe me when I tell you, she will be treated better by Riyaz than she ever would have been where she was headed. But it is not my story to tell."

"Do you love her?"

She hated herself for asking the question. His dark eyes went flinty. Hard. "Love is not a factor for me. For anything."

It wasn't a denial. "Do you love her?" she repeated.

He shook his head. "I can't love. Not in the way that you mean. I'm sorry. If that sounds hard to you…"

"No. It's exactly what I would expect. And I received that better than hearing that you love another woman, actually. So thank you."

"I told you. I told you what my priorities were. You didn't believe me."

"I just thought at some point the human element would matter. Me. Brianna."

"My brother spent sixteen years in a dungeon. He is the human element for me. I…"

She saw something tortured in his eyes then. Dark and pained. "I might have devoted my life to freeing the country. But he had no life. None at all. He didn't even have the honor of being the one to free the country. It is… It is not something that I can ignore. It is not something that I can simply let go. I owe my brother years that he cannot get back."

"You didn't hold him in captivity."

His gaze became bleak. "You don't know what I carry. And it is of no consequence. For I must now support the throne. I must now support Riyaz. If he wants Brianna, he can have her. For my part, I have you."

He turned and began to walk down the corridor. The palace was as she remembered it. Golden stone inlay on the walls and the floors. The ceilings. It was familiar and yet somehow alien all at once.

And they were to be living here. Somehow, she had ended up in this palace anyway.

And she realized on some level that… That he had chosen her over Riyaz. For all that he professed to have no feeling. For all that he professed Riyaz to be the most important thing… He had chosen her.

And he simply wouldn't take something from his brother again.

Did that indicate that he didn't care for her?

He pushed open the door, and she followed him. It was a sitting room, luxuriously appointed. "My chambers there," he said, gesturing to the left. "Yours are there."

"We're to have separate rooms?"

"It is how things are done."

It was not how they had done things last night. They had slept wrapped around each other. In that bed in the desert. But it was as if everything had changed. Between then and now.

"You must be tired. You should sleep."

"I'm not tired…"

"Then perhaps I am. In the next couple of days a great many things will unfold. You must have your strength saved up. For we will go public. As a restored royal family. And as husband and wife."

"Well. I guess… That will take some strength."

"And I did promise you a computer and a phone. You will be given those things. You may return to work."

She knew that should make her feel something. Happy. Excited.

She didn't. Instead, she went to bed alone. And while that should have been normal, it already felt wrong. And even though she knew she was with the right man, everything else felt wrong. And she didn't know what to do about it.

CHAPTER FOURTEEN

IT WAS LATE. *He had helped Ariel sneak back into the palace. They should never have been out like they were. There would be hell to pay if they were discovered. His father would lecture him soundly on risking Ariel's reputation.*

They were not children anymore. At fourteen, they would be held accountable for their actions. And people would be suspicious that their behavior had been inappropriate.

A smile curved his lips. He looked up at the desert sky.

"Ariel."

He had wanted to behave inappropriately with her. But he hadn't. Mostly because he would not subject her to any sort of censure. He cared for her so deeply. She was... The moon. That guiding light in the darkness.

He turned and began to walk back toward the palace. There was a door that could al-

ways be opened no matter the time of night. A way that he could sneak in. Undetected. It was the way that he had sent Ariel earlier.

"Cairo?"

He turned sharply to see Ariel's father standing there.

"Mr. Hart."

"Your Highness. I'm sorry to startle you. It's only that... I have not seen Ariel."

Ariel should have been back safely in bed by now. But it was possible her father had missed her.

"I... I saw her out here, sir. We had gone for a walk. But I saw her safely back inside the palace."

"I see," her dad said, his eyes taking on a suspicious light. "You know... It could be taken the wrong way. The two of you out here walking together. She is supposed to marry Riyaz..."

"She's my friend," said Cairo. "There's nothing more to it."

"I will take you at your word. Of course. You are part of the royal family after all. Known for their integrity."

He nodded, feeling relieved. "I'm being honest. You don't... You won't tell my father?"

"No. There's no need to speak to your father. Though... I cannot figure out how to get

back into the palace. I left to find Ariel. And now... I do not wish to wake the staff trying to gain entrance. I assume there's a way?"

"There's a passage. Through the garden. I can show you how I get in."

Cairo woke up in a cold sweat. The memory that had played through his subconscious was one that he had done his best to banish.

He knew well how they had gotten into the palace. The enemies of his father. A word from Ariel's.

But where had Ariel's father gotten his intel? From Cairo. It was Cairo who had destroyed his family. Cairo who had dishonored them so. In his weakness for Ariel, and in his desire to stay out of trouble he had been the one that had caused all of this.

And yet again Ariel had been his weakness. It was... Unacceptable.

It's your fault.

Yes. But nobody ever had to know. It would help no one. It would fix nothing. He didn't even like himself to know. He had spent all these years trying to fix it. All these years trying to make it right.

It was being back here that had brought it all up again.

He despised it.

And yet here he was, to live with the woman who tested his every weakness.

But love? He did not possess the ability for that. Not anymore. And nothing else mattered but what happened next. He had not been right. He had not been what his brother needed, but he would be now. He would give Riyaz whatever he needed. He would... He would fight. He would give up his life for his country. For his brother.

And yet you took Ariel. And you managed very neatly not to think about how when given the chance to betray Riyaz again you did.

It was done now. It was done, and Riyaz lusted after another woman anyway. What did it matter?

He thought of going to Ariel. Burying his sorrow in his desire for her.

But he would not allow himself that. Would not allow himself that escape.

Ariel threw herself into work. She had been sad last night that Cairo hadn't come to her bed, but she couldn't wallow in that. She needed to get on with it. She had gotten on her email for the first time in a few weeks, and had begun to go through everything that she had missed. Made sure everybody knew that she wasn't dead. She had spun a story about reuniting with an old boyfriend. And how they'd had a whirlwind romance and marriage.

She was pretty proud of herself. PR wasn't necessarily her thing, but this was definitely a stunning example of some pretty genius PR.

But she wished that the story were true. She realized that for her it was. That she had reunited with the single most important man in her life, and it had seemed the most clear and obvious thing in the world to fall into his arms. To fall into his bed. To speak vows to him.

And she didn't know what he was thinking at all. She had thought that maybe they were on the same page. She had thought that perhaps they wanted the same things. She didn't know now.

You know that you don't want the same things. Because you care for him in a way that he has said he will never care for you. That was true. And it hurt to acknowledge it herself. But she wasn't going to lie to herself about it either. She wasn't half so fragile. She had already lived more than one life. A life where she had been certain she would end up living in this palace married to the sheikh. A life where she had fallen in love with the boy that she wasn't meant to love. Yes. She had already lived more than one reality.

She had been free in Paris. And yet, she had never come into this sort of freedom. She had been free in Paris, and yet it still hadn't felt like her life.

This felt much closer.

But still…

He didn't come to her bed again that night. Or in the days following. In the interim, she was subjected to married beauty treatments. Prepared for her public unveil as Cairo's wife. But it was more than that. They were revealing to Nazul for the first time that Cairo and Riyaz lived.

And that they were back in power.

She had thought that perhaps Brianna was being prepared for an unveil as well, but on the day, when she had been wrapped in sensuous silks, her hair done, her makeup applied to perfection, and she saw Brianna wearing her sweats, she knew that that was not actually the plan.

"You are not making your debut with Riyaz?"

"No. I believe that he will be waiting until the wedding that I have not yet agreed to."

"What do you have to go back to? I mean, what life is he asking you to leave behind?"

Her face went distant. "I… I don't have much. I have my business. I had… Cairo. As my friend. And I suppose that he is here now."

"It's the principle," said Ariel, hoping that she sounded like she was on the other woman's team. It would do no good to have there be division between them. When she walked back into the apartment, her heart stopped. For there was Cairo, standing there in full military uniform. A navy blue high collared jacket, a scabbard at his waist. He looked fearsome and glorious. And she wanted to cling to him and let the entire world know that this man, this dangerous looking man belonged to her. She marveled at the impulse. At the way that he made her feel.

It was the most brilliantly absurd thing.

She had never thought herself drawn to dangerous men. And yet…

Perhaps it was because she knew of the danger and destruction that had occurred here. But it made her feel… Good. Good to know that he could protect her if need be. Good to know that he would be the one looking out for her.

She was dressed in white. And she knew why now. Because they would make a beautiful contrasting picture standing together. And

the idea had been to make her look somewhat bridal.

"Are you ready?"

"Yes," he said. "I've been ready for this
moment for the last sixteen years. The question is… Are you?"

"I think we both know that the question
is… Is Riyaz?"

A knowing look passed between them, and
for a moment, she felt like they were a couple
again. Like they were in some kind of unity.

She walked over to him and took his arm.
And they walked from the room together. She
wanted to melt into him. Into this moment.

"We will be standing on the balcony, where
Riyaz will make a speech. As will I. You will
stand to my right."

She nodded.

"I don't have to speak, do I?"

"No. You don't."

"That's good."

Though, she had the vague idea that she
should ask if she was even allowed to speak.
She wondered if she would like his answer
to that question. She imagined not. They
stepped out onto the corridor, and there was
Riyaz. Standing there alone. He was wearing a loose white tunic, and white pants. His
dark hair was long and loose. He still had a

full beard, scars that spoke of immeasurable cruelties that he suffered at the hands of the guards here.

"Riyaz," she said.

"Ariel," he said.

They had not spoken directly since she had come back to the palace.

"I hope that you know," she said, "you have my loyalty."

"Yes. I do know. But my brother has you."

"Yes. He does. But he… He always has, Riyaz. I don't know if you know that."

He looked between the two of them, his gaze sharp. "Has he?"

"We will discuss it later," said Cairo. "For now we have a kingdom to reclaim."

They were the same height, and Cairo had lean muscle. She knew he was fast and agile.

Riyaz looked like a weapon in the form of a man. He did not have a sword at his waist, and yet, she had the sense that he did not need one. That he would be more than happy to take on any enemies with his bare hands. And that he would prefer it that way.

He was built like a beast.

And she had the feeling that between the two of them, a beleaguered nation would feel comforted knowing they had two kinds of lethal men at the helm.

They stepped out onto the balcony, and a ripple went through the crowd. She wondered how many of them had heard through rumor that this would happen. She knew that of course Cairo's people already knew. So there must have been some rumors that had made their way back over the border.

Whispers. But of course it would be hard to believe if you didn't see it with your own eyes.

"The al Hadid family is back on the throne," said Riyaz, his voice strong and clear.

Ariel turned and looked behind her just briefly. And she saw Brianna looking out from the shadows. She looked nervous. Then she looked very much like she cared how well Riyaz fared.

She did love him. Not Cairo. But Riyaz.

That made Ariel feel much better.

Whatever was happening between the two of them might be complicated, but it was not insurmountable.

And it was clear that Riyaz was the man that Brianna wanted.

"You will remember that years ago my family was betrayed. By a militia that rose up here, but also by the betrayal of the Hart family."

The words slammed into Ariel's chest. She

had not been prepared for him to mention her family.

"Ariel Hart was promised to be my bride at the time, and her father took money to betray my parents. But we have done work to restore that which was destroyed. We will not live in the past. We will not live for revenge. My brother, Sheikh Cairo al Hadid, has taken her as his wife. I myself will take a bride in the coming weeks. But that will be a separate announcement for a separate time. You are free. And the indignities that you have suffered these long years will not go on. We will move forward. Strong and united. With my brother at the head of the military, we will also be undefeated. We will be victorious."

And now it was Cairo's turn.

"My brother addressed the betrayal of the Hart family. And we want to make sure that you know that we stand with you. We do not forget the indignity that you have suffered. Riyaz himself was chained up in a dungeon the last sixteen years. But he survived. For the sake of this country. So it is not lightly that we reconcile in this moment. But it is essential that we do so. But we cannot live in the past. Here in the darkness. My marriage to Ariel is a representation of all that we can be. All that we will overcome." He kissed her hand. Right there in front of the crowd, and it sent her heart soaring. The people cheered, and the royal family left the balcony. And she knew that this would be a day that would live in the history of this country forever.

This was the light at the end of a very dark tunnel. And she felt nothing but pride at the way that Cairo had made this happen.

It was so easy to get bound up in the personal component of the past. What her father had done.

And it was easy to not fully give credit to the work that Cairo had done to heal it. To heal all of this.

He had been tireless. But he had made this moment happen. He had.

And she...

She chose him. She chose this life. This life that this man had fought so hard for. These people that he had never forgotten. His brother that he would never abandon.

She admired all of it so. She... She loved him.

The simple truth was she had a life made of freedom. All of the freedom that she could possibly desire. Her father hadn't been in her life anymore, and her mother hadn't really either. It had been up to her to do whatever she wanted. And she had... She had never fully moved on from Cairo. She couldn't have him. She didn't want anybody. And as she looked at her husband's profile, she dimly wondered if he had done similar, just opposite. If he couldn't have her he would have everybody. And maybe that was aggrandizing her a bit, but she couldn't let go of the fact that consistently, she was his weakness. Consistently, she was the area where he did not put his brother before everything else.

It made her smile. Even if just slightly.

And it made her certain. That no matter what he had said... No matter what he claimed about loving her...

She loved him. She loved him with all that she was. And she wanted... She wanted him.

Forever.

This wasn't Stockholm syndrome. She had fallen in love with him when they were children. They were fated. And so many people had stepped in the way to try and keep them from happening. To keep their love from being fully realized. But they didn't allow it.

She wouldn't allow it.

Circumstances might have made him hard and dark. Circumstances might have made it difficult for him to know what love was, but that did not mean that she should lose hope. Because for sixteen years, she had carried a candle for him. For sixteen years he had been the only thing. And if a separation, the presumption of death couldn't banish that, she wouldn't let anything else destroy it either.

She felt dizzy. Like she had made vows yet again. Like this was a renewal in her soul. Something that she hadn't anticipated. She had loved him. Of course she had. For all these years. From the time she was a girl she had loved him. She had loved him with all that she was.

But this was... Admitting it. Claiming it. And owning her piece of it. Even if she could leave now, she wouldn't. She was not a prisoner, because she was deciding she wasn't a prisoner, not because of what Cairo had given her. Not because of anything other than her own choice.

She was choosing this. Choosing him.

But when it was time for them to go to bed again that night, he did not come to her room. And when she went to his... He wasn't there.

CHAPTER FIFTEEN

CAIRO HAD TAKEN to pacing the halls at night. He was in no fit state to go to Ariel's bed, and he knew it. And yet he craved her. With all that he was.

Tonight, as he roamed around sleepless, he heard footsteps. They were not hers. They were hard and heavy. Decisive.

"Riyaz?"

His brother seemed to appear from the shadows. "Yes."

"You don't sleep either?"

"Not conventionally."

His brother offered no explanation for that cryptic statement, and so Cairo did not ask.

"Perhaps it is this place," Cairo said. "Perhaps there are too many ghosts here."

"This is the only place I've been, for sixteen years. This is the only place I have been. And it is the only place I will ever be. For now I am the sheikh. So where will I go?"

Guilt assaulted Cairo. "I'm sorry," he said.

"For what?"

"It feels wrong. That I spent all those years out there. And you spent them in here."

"It's not as if you chose it, any more than I did."

"Still…"

"Do not play the part of regretful younger brother now. You were happy to make the decision to marry Ariel."

"You don't want her."

"No. I don't."

"Then why bring it up?"

"We've been separated for sixteen years. And I've been alone in a dungeon. I had no one to tease."

He looked at his brother. "Are you teasing me?"

"I think so. I spent a great many years not able to smile or laugh. But sometimes now I do. It is interesting."

And he knew then that what he really wanted for Riyaz was for him to leave all those years behind. He also knew that it was probably functionally impossible for his brother to do so. There had been so much pain. So much abuse.

So much solitude. And yet, he was speaking better now.

"I heard that you did not sleep in a bed. Have you now?"

And there was a slight grin on his brother's face.

"Yes. I have."

"But do you. Routinely?" It was clear by the look on his brother's face that when he was in a bed he was not alone.

"Sleep? No. But I have not learned to enjoy softness. I don't know that I ever will…fully be comfortable in it though."

"We should have traded places," he said, his voice rough.

Regret rose up inside of him. If he hadn't have told Ariel's father where that door was…

"It was not a question of should. Or a question of what we wanted. It's what happened. Carry your demons. I'll carry mine. We do not need to shoulder one another's."

And on that note, his brother turned and began to walk away from him. "You have a woman in your bed," he said. "So do I. Why are we in hallways?"

"I don't know."

Except he did know. He was staying away from her because… Because things had begun to feel complicated. Here. In this place. Where he could not ignore the truth of what he had done.

Of what he deserved.

He had taken her. And he had no right to do so. And it was only a happy accident that Riyaz had found a woman that he preferred. Otherwise...

He gritted his teeth and turned abruptly, going back to his apartment, to his room.

And when he pushed open the door, she was there.

She was sitting on the edge of the bed, naked, her sheet barely obscuring her glorious curves. "What are you doing in here?"

"Waiting for you," she said.

She shifted, and the sheet fell just between her thighs, covering the triangle of curls there. But her hips were exposed. She only just had her breasts covered with the edge of the white fabric.

And a kick of lust overtook him. Except... There was something more. Something deeper. And he rejected it. Wholly.

"I'm not in the mood."

"Everything about you suggests otherwise," she said, dropping the sheet and letting it slither down her curves.

For all that she had been a virgin when he had first laid with her, she had never had any sort of embarrassment about her body. Which he appreciated. She was beautiful, and she had nothing to be ashamed of, but he could certainly use a little bit of it right now. Because this… This restless display of all her glory was pushing against things he could not afford to have challenged.

He was too much on edge.

This was supposed to be his redemption arc. And had he not destroyed it already by taking her as his wife? Certainly, he could rewrite the story, certainly, things had worked out better than he could have anticipated, because of the fact that Riyaz clearly had an attachment to Brianna. But he had not known that.

He could not be redeemed. That was the problem.

And yet… There she was. Looking like temptation personified. Like everything he wanted.

And he did not think that he could turn away. Why?

He had proven that there was no redemption in sight for him. No change. The best that he could hope for was to fling himself on the altar of service to his brother. Because as far as his soul went? It was selfish. It always had been. It was selfishness that had driven him to give her father that information out in the courtyard. It was selfishness and the need to stay out of trouble. It was selfishness that had him out in the desert with Ariel in the first place.

Because the gravest sin had been what she had been about even before her father had approached him. When he had taken her into the room with the jewels. When he had let himself fantasize about making her his wife. And then what had he done? Years and years and years of working to reclaim the throne, to get Riyaz what he wanted, and instead, he had claimed her for himself.

His soul was hollow. It was corrupt. And there was nothing else that he could ever be. Nothing. The idea that he could be…

It was nothing more than a vague fantasy. But she was not a vague fantasy. She was here. In the flesh. Smooth and tempting and lovely and everything that he wanted.

And so he would have her. He would have her now. In his bed, because had he not already committed the unpardonable sins?

Yes, he had. Already he'd taken her. Already, his actions had seen his brother in prison for sixteen years. Already his weakness had seen his mother slaughtered on the tile floor of the throne room. Already his cowardice had caused the death of his father.

His father who had fought until the end, while he had run away.

He was already these things.

And if he was going to be a sinner, then he might as well revel in it. Might as well glory in the iniquity. For what else was to be done?

He had sought to become better. Sought to become more honorable, but even in his pursuit of bringing back the power to the throne, he had been nothing but a hedonistic playboy. He could tell himself all manner of stories about why he had done these things, but some of it had been to glory in the freedom of being away from the soul. Some of it had been to glory in the fact that he was not in his traditional country where his moves would be watched. Some of it was reveling in the fact that he was alive. And the fact that he was not in chains.

What a grave sin it was.

There was no coming back from it.

The idea that he'd ever thought he could was laughable. And so why?

He knelt down in front of the bed and growled, forcing her legs apart, moving the sheet to the side and exposing the glistening heart of her to his gaze.

She was glorious. Pink and glistening and

lovely. And he wanted to taste her. Dive deep into all that she was to satisfy his need.

He reached around and grabbed her buttocks, pulling her toward his mouth and licking her like he was a starving man. She gasped, and he pressed two fingers inside of her, loving the way she quivered beneath his touch.

She rocked against him and he tasted her, deep and long, curving his fingers as they thrust in and out of her, taking every cry of pleasure and bringing out yet more.

She was his. His to pleasure. His to corrupt. She had done this to him. Her. She was why. She was part of it. She was not innocent in this. She had known what she was doing to him. Always. She had tempted him. She was the one who had taken her clothing off back at his house. She had wanted it as much as he did. And she should suffer here in the depths with him.

If they were both to die of pleasure, then it would be no less than they deserved.

But it was a hell he would gladly burn in.

She cried out, pulsing, her orgasm making her shake.

He withdrew his fingers and lifted her up onto the bed, putting her on all fours, smoothing his hands down the elegant line of her spine, bringing one down to cup her rear before slapping her once, making her gasp.

"I wonder how many years it will take for me to cease to be able to shock you," he said. "I quite enjoy it. Your innocence is a novelty."

She looked over her shoulder at him, aqua eyes reaching down into his soul. "A novelty?"

"Yes. I wonder how long it will last."

He slapped her again, this time on the other side, and she yelped. Then he pushed two fingers into her from behind, testing her readiness at this angle.

He gripped her hips and pressed himself forward before he thrust hard.

Then with one hand he pressed between her shoulder blades, pushing her head down so that she could not look at him. He didn't wish to see her face.

How many times had he had sex like this? In this position?

Countless.

She could be anyone. She didn't matter. It was just more sex. Just more sin. And what was a little bit more? What was a little bit more when you were already hell bound?

He thrust into her blindly, chasing at the pleasure that he craved. The peak. The oblivion. This had been his life for sixteen years.

Oblivion. Anything to block out the truth of it. Then he could pretend that he was on a mission. A benevolent one. With breaks for pleasure in between. But the reality was, he knew that he was the center. He knew that he was the murderer. The weak one. The straw that had broken the entire camel's back. He was the one that had caused all of this. It was his duty to try and make up for it. As much as he never could.

It was his calling.

The thing that he had to strive for.

Because it had all been his fault.

His mother's blood. His father's cries of agony as he had tried to avenge her, tried to protect them all.

And worst of all—yes, *worst*, because at least his parents had the benefit of being in the afterlife—had been Riyaz.

In chains.

Yes. He had tried to block these things out. He had tried to pretend that these things were not down to him.

Oblivion. He just needed oblivion. Except he could not get it.

Not without picturing her. Not without it being her.

She tossed her hair back, that pale, distinct hair, and squeezed him tight, and he knew.

"Ariel," he growled.

And he felt her shudder as he said her name. He felt his entire body arrive in spasms of pleasure. And he had done her a disservice, for he had not yet made her come.

He pushed his hand down between her thighs and thrust hard into her as his orgasm overtook him completely. He roared, and just as he did, he felt her pulse around him. Felt her climax.

And then she collapsed onto the bed, breathing hard.

His wife.

His beautiful wife. It could not be denied and neither could she.

It was Ariel. Only Ariel. His downfall. His muse. His everything.

"Cairo," she whispered. "Cairo, I love you."

And everything inside of him went dark.

CHAPTER SIXTEEN

THERE WAS SOMETHING possessed inside of her husband, and Ariel had no idea what it was. But he wasn't himself.

What even was himself? She didn't know. She thought that she knew him, but ever since they had returned here... He had been a stranger to her. Not coming to her bed, and then tonight... It was like he was running from demons. And she didn't know why. She didn't know what was hurting him so badly. Didn't know why he was distant, and yet intense all at once. It was like he wanted to draw nearer to her and also pull away forever all at the same time.

She simply couldn't understand.

"Tell me," she said. "Tell me what's wrong."

But he had still said nothing since she had said that she loved him. He wasn't speaking at all. He was just sitting there, his breath rising and falling harshly.

"Cairo," she whispered.

"No," he denied viciously.

"Cairo, I just want… I love you."

"You don't know what you're speaking of. You know nothing of love. Your father betrayed my family. He would have sold you as well if it suited him. He practically did. He didn't care what you thought of it, didn't care what your mother thought. How long would it have taken for him to sell you to the next highest bidder? He did so when he brought you to be engaged to my brother, did he not? What do you know of love? Has anyone in your life ever loved you?"

He spoke to wound. And his words hit their mark.

No, her father had been selfish. Her mother had been passive.

Even though her mother may have loved her, it wasn't an active sort of love.

It wasn't a love that helped or healed.

"You say that as if I've never thought of it. But of course I have. Of course I've wondered if my father ever loved me. Of course I've wondered why the bond between myself and my mother was so easily broken. Of course I have. But I do know what love is, Cairo. I have known. Since I was a girl of twelve. Maybe even younger. I have known that it was you. And when you were gone… Well, I couldn't love anyone else. I tried. I hoped. I was open to it, but it never happened. It never happened because I couldn't want anybody but you. And it never happened because you formed my concept of what desire was."

"And that is all it is," he said. "It's just sex. Good sex, but sex, nonetheless. It isn't love, my moon, and it never will be."

"Why? Because you don't believe in it? And why is that? What is love if not a sixteen-year pursuit to free your brother? That is love."

"That is atonement," he said, the words sounding torn from him.

"What?"

"You heard what I said, do not question it. You require no explanation. You are bound to me, and we do not need to come to an agreement on these things. But you do not need to tell me that you love me. Never again."

She sat there, her heart thundering hard. She thought that it would break into a thousand pieces.

Shatter.

And maybe she would shatter along with it.

She knew her father had died of a heart attack, and it had nothing to do with emotions. But what if it had?

Was it his guilt? Thundering around inside of his chest? Was she going to suffer the same fate?

It certainly felt like it. At least right now. As badly as it all hurt.

Except… No. Because what he was saying didn't make any sense. "Why bar me from saying it? I'm not asking you to say it in return. In fact, I'm asking nothing from you. All I'm asking is what you have already given. I am offering love. I love you. And I always have."

"No," he responded. "This is not negotiable. It is not sensible. You are acting foolish."

"Why? Because, actually, the thing is you've identified the problem with my father. He didn't love anyone but himself. He didn't love anyone but money. So why would you reject the idea of love? Love is what prevents these things from happening."

"No," he said, gripping her arms. "Love creates these situations. You know I fancied myself in love with you when I was a boy. A boy of fourteen. I wanted… Everything. With you. To kiss you, to lose myself inside of you. I wanted to learn what passion was with you. I wanted to steal you from my brother. I wanted you to be mine. All mine.

"I wanted it more than anything else in the

world, and I risked your reputation running around the palace with you as I did. Running around out in the desert as we did."

"My reputation was never compromised."

"Nearly was. Or at least, I thought so. That last night, out in the desert, when you begged me to show you… That last night I met your father there. He knew. He knew that we had been out together. He couldn't find you and he questioned me on it."

"I didn't… I never knew. I had no idea that he had checked in on me…" She was confused. Because it was difficult to remember anything about that night except for being out with Cairo. Certainly not any interaction she might've had with her father.

"He met me outside in the dark. He made it very clear that he knew we were together. And he forced me to confess it besides. He also made it very clear that it would be bad if anyone found out. And then he asked me… He asked me to show him a way into the palace. One where he wouldn't have to disturb the staff. I agreed."

"Cairo…"

"That is how the invaders ended up getting into the castle. That is how my family was murdered. Your father gave them that information. It was his power. His leverage.

He got it from me. Why? Because you and I were sneaking around together. Because even though we didn't kiss, even though we didn't make love, we might as well have. We compromised everything. I compromised everything. Because I was afraid. Afraid of getting in trouble. Afraid of losing time with you. Don't you see? It was that weakness that got everyone killed."

"No," she said. "It wasn't. It wasn't you. It was my father. It was his willingness to manipulate a boy and his feelings. He was willing to get you to give that information knowing that it would get you killed. Knowing it would cost your entire family their lives. Believe me, he did not care about the consequences. And he likely thought that you would be dead as well and there would be no regret for you because you would be in the ground. It is by luck and good fortune that you escaped. But you didn't cause it. He did. He betrayed you."

"No," he said. "He did not. I betrayed us all."

"That is ridiculous."

"It is a heaviness that I have lived with all these years. And I… I will never love you. I will never love anything. Because it could cost the safety of this nation. Already I allowed my desire for you to cloud my judgment. That is how we arrived here. You were meant for Riyaz."

"No," she said. "I was never for Riyaz." She shook her head again. "It was you. Only you. Always you. Do you not know?" She stepped forward and touched his face, his beautiful face. "Do you not know?"

He closed his eyes. "Riyaz was in captivity all this time..."

"You have been in captivity. You're enslaved to this. To this guilt that you feel, but you didn't do this."

He wrapped his hands around her wrists and pulled her hands away from his face. And then he stepped away from her. "You pity the wrong person."

And then he walked out of the room and left her alone there.

Left her alone with her heartbreak.

And she knew that it was up to her. Whether she would allow it to destroy her, or whether she would find a way to be strong.

CHAPTER SEVENTEEN

HE RODE OUT in the darkness, his horse's hooves kicking up sand, the echo of the hoofbeats sounding in his soul.

She'd looked at him and she'd pitied him. Felt sorry for him. Wouldn't allow him to accept his guilt.

And she...

She thought that he was a prisoner.

But no. She was.

I love you.

How could she love him? Not only did she not truly know who he was, not only did she not truly know the perils of his character... But...

You have failed again. You have failed in a way you haven't seen. For it was not just Riyaz... It was her.

He had taken away her freedom.

She had begged him not to make her prisoner, and he had done so anyway. And he had told himself that allowing her access to a computer made her free?

And now she said she loved him. What insanity was this? Would he ever not be a monster? Would anything about him ever be right?

There, deep in the desert with nothing around him, he let out a primal growl that seemed to vibrate the earth around him.

It was grief, and it was regret. For all the damage he had caused. For all that he could not put back together.

Except you can. You can set her free.

Because whose atonement had she ever been? Certainly not the country's. And not Riyaz's. He had wanted her, and he had brought her back here.

At first, it had been to prove himself to his brother, a salve for his guilt. And a way to punish himself.

But then... Then it had been about having her. Possessing her. Regardless of what she wanted.

And he might be a monster beyond redemption.

For he had proven his own selfishness at every turn. He would never be able to restore the sixteen years of Riyaz's life that had been lost. He could not bring his parents back from the dead.

He could not allow himself to love Ariel.

Or rather…

He did love her. But he needed her to not be near him. And if he really wanted to do the right thing, he needed to allow her freedom.

He had to send her away.

He rode, far and hard away from the palace, and by the time he returned, the sun was rising. He had not slept.

He didn't need to.

He was resolved.

He dismounted the horse, and a servant came to relieve him of the animal.

Then he pushed open the double doors to the palace and began to walk toward his and Ariel's apartment.

He opened the door, and then saw her there, sitting on the couch, in a robe. Looking as if she had sat there all night.

"Get dressed," he said.

She looked up at him, her eyes red.

"I'm quite enjoying a slow morning," she said.

"You must prepare yourself."

"What's happening?"

"You are going back to Paris."

"What?"

"You're going back."

"I didn't ask to go back," she said.

"And I did not ask you what you wanted. I will not hold you here. I will no longer tie you to this family. Or to a past that… Was not your fault."

"I know it isn't my fault," she said. "But you don't. You don't know it isn't your fault. And now what are you doing? Punishing yourself?"

"I am making things right. This is the only thing that I can set to rights."

"I chose you," she said. "Don't you understand? I chose you, Cairo. If I hadn't… Don't you think I would've had a lover in these last sixteen years? But it was always you. I had freedom. I had freedom to be with whoever I wanted, and I didn't want to. Because I could never get you out of my heart. I had a choice. And now… Kidnapped or not, you are my clear choice."

"No," he said. "You will not be another in my long list of sins, Ariel."

"And you think that sending me away and acting like none of this ever happened will… Absolve you? You're just afraid. You're afraid of what you feel for me. And you're making it about me… It isn't fair."

"I will carry you out to the private jet myself."

"A reverse coup and a reverse kidnapping. You really have had a busy few weeks."

"You think I'm kidding."

And he could see something change in her face. Some kind of acceptance. Some kind of resolve. "You need me to do this."

"No. You need to do this."

"No. You need me to. And so I will. I will prove to you that I love you."

"Didn't you hear what I told you about what happened?"

"Is that why you're telling me? To prove to me that you don't deserve to be loved? It's too bad for you, because I think that you are. Because I care about you. I like you, and I love you. And I always have. What an inconvenience for you." She stood up. "But I'm going to get dressed. I'm going to get on the plane. And in two days I'm going to come back. I'm going to buy a plane ticket, and I'm going to show up at the palace. Unless you want to come find me beforehand. To ask me to stay with you. Not kidnap me. Not make demands. You know where I live."

And she began to collect her things. And he simply watched.

And then, in only an hour, she was gone. In the air, headed back to Paris.

And he found himself walking, stumbling, out of the apartment. And down into the dungeon.

She was broken. Possibly irrevocably. Possibly forever.

By the time the plane landed in Paris, and she got in the car that took her back to her apartment, the apartment that she had been so sorry to leave just weeks before, she felt like she was so brittle she might fall apart.

He didn't love her. So maybe it was a foolish thing, to think of buying a plane ticket and going back.

But she didn't know how else to show him. To make him believe that she was choosing him.

But what she wanted... What she really wanted was for him to choose her. What she really wanted was for him to understand.

Yes, he had given her father information that her father had misused, but it wasn't his fault that her father had betrayed them.

But she didn't really think that was the problem either. She just thought it was fear. A feeling of not being enough. And she knew what that felt like. Because she... She had always felt like that. Her father had used her to maneuver politically, and her mother had sort of dropped out of her life.

She knew what that was like.

But being with him, experiencing the intensity of their connection, it made her feel more than enough. She was so brave when she was with him. So much more herself than she'd ever been.

She craved it. She wanted it back. She wanted to be with him.

But at the same time she knew that she would always take that forward with her. Wherever she went.

She might not be with him. But she would always be with him.

But she hoped. She truly hoped that he would come for her.

He had told her once that it took hope to save Riyaz.

And she needed hope now.

Badly.

The dungeon was where his brother found him. Laid out like a sacrifice to enemies who were no longer there.

"What the hell are you doing?"

He looked up into the darkness. "I am seeing what it was like for you."

"Well. I still sleep down here. So you might ask before you enter."

"Why do you sleep down here?"

"Because you don't change immediately," said Riyaz. "I hate it here. And yet for many years it was the only place I saw. There is a safety to it. But it is captivity." He could hear his brother move toward him, sit down on the bench beside him. "But then. Everything is a cage of some kind. None of us are truly free."

"No," he said.

"I know that Ariel left. Why?"

"Because I told her to."

"I see. And why would you do that? You want to keep her."

"Look at where we are, Riyaz. We are in a dungeon. Do you really think it appropriate to keep a woman in the palace against her will? Even if it is in my bed and not a dungeon?"

"Did she say she didn't want to be with you?"

"No. But, she didn't have the choice to come here in the first place. Not now, and not all those years ago. She doesn't even know what she wants."

Riyaz laughed. "Is it her that doesn't know what she wants? Or is it you?"

"And what about you? You are keeping a woman prisoner as well."

"Have I expressed a moral difficulty with this?"

"I would think that you of all people would."

"Why?"

He had nothing to say to that. His brother didn't simply know… What was there to be said?

"Do you want her?" Riyaz asked him.

"Ariel? Of course. I have upended everything to have her. I betrayed you. Again."

"What do you mean again?"

"You said that we should keep our demons to ourselves, Riyaz. But I think you should know about mine. I was in love with Ariel when we were children. And I used to sneak out with her. When we were fourteen we went out into the desert. And we were caught. I was. By her father. And he asked me a question… And I answered it. To keep myself from being in trouble. I gave him an easier way to get into the palace. I did not feel as if I could tell him no. He would… He would reveal what happened between myself and Ariel."

"So you're the reason they came into the palace."

"Yes," he said.

"That was a very stupid thing to do," said Riyaz.

He didn't deny Cairo's fault the way that Ariel had.

"It was," Cairo agreed.

"Fourteen-year-old boys are stupid."

"Yes. And you were sixteen. And suffered greatly for my stupidity."

"They were intent on killing the royal family, they would've done it somehow. Even if it'd been exploding a motorcade. It would've occurred. This was a neat and clean way to do it, but... They would've found a way."

"Are you trying to absolve me?"

"No. Your actions led to that event. But you cannot control the intent of others. So, yes, something that you did played a part in the way they were able to kill our parents and take me prisoner. But... I believe it would've happened either way. And perhaps we would've been blown up."

"You can't know that."

"No. But you can't know otherwise."

"I don't understand," Cairo said. "Are you blaming me? Forgiving me?"

"I can't do either. Here is one thing you learn with only yourself for company for a great number of years. The world turns regardless of your involvement in it. In the dark of night, you have only yourself. And the only way you can be rescued is if there is someone out there

MAISEY YATES

who cares enough to do it. I can't absolve you. You have to absolve yourself. But you are the person who came for me. Whether you are blameless or not... That is something."

It wasn't a rousing speech of forgiveness. It was something deeper than that. It was something that Cairo could actually...accept.

Neither of them were perfect. But they were here together in the dark. He had come for Riyaz when Riyaz needed him. And now Riyaz had come for him. And perhaps they could never make fair the things that were unfair. And perhaps they could never make whole the things that were broken.

And perhaps he could never be redeemed.

But maybe... Maybe he could be loved. Just as he was anyway. Because wasn't that what Riyaz was giving him? Not absolution, and not blame. Just acceptance.

"I have to go to her," he said.

"Of course you do," said Riyaz.

"I'm not taking her prisoner."

"I wouldn't care if you were."

"Yes. I know." And he decided that he would not challenge his brother on that. That was for him and Brianna to work out, and he had a feeling they would. At least eventually.

But Riyaz's woman was not his problem. He had to go and get his own.

CHAPTER EIGHTEEN

SHE HAD BOUGHT the tickets. She was leaving tomorrow. If he didn't come...

If he didn't come she would be devastated. But she would go to him. She would show him.

She would show him what she had chosen.

She went to the window and looked out at the Parisian skyline. And that was when she saw him.

Run.

The word echoed in her soul. She flung the door to the apartment open and began to run down the stairs, all the way down to the street, and by the time she got there, he was just about to approach the door.

"Cairo," she said.

"Ariel."

And she found herself in his arms. Kissing him.

When he pulled away, his breathing was

ragged. "Ariel," he said. "I've come for you. My brother did not magically forgive me. And I am not immediately redeemed. I am not a different man than the one that you left behind. But I am... Willing. I am willing to accept what you have offered me. You came to me while I was in the dark. You came to rescue me. To lift me out. And I want it. I want your love. And I want to reach out and take your hand and give you my love in return. I was afraid... Because... Of what I felt loving you had cost before. But really, it wasn't that. It was just knowing what it feels like to lose you. And wanting to never lose you again. And so... I cut you off myself. As if that made it better. But the problem is... I don't know what makes things better. I know how to fight. And I know how to embrace oblivion. But you... You are peace. And you are sharp and clear. And you are quite different from anything that I have ever had. I'm not sure I know how to love. But I want to."

"Oh, my sun," she said. "Don't you know that you burned so bright? Don't you know that you've known how to love me since you were a boy? It's as natural as breathing to us. We couldn't stop if we tried."

"You're right," he said, as if it was the most wondrous thing. A revelation.

Her heart hurt. With joy. With pain for him. With hope.

"We never need to be shown. Not by anyone. It was simply part of us."

"Fate," he said.

"Fate we had to choose," she said, stepping toward him and taking his hand in hers. "I want to go home now. To Nazul. Take me to the desert."

EPILOGUE

IT TOOK A number of years for Cairo to feel as if he had fully forgiven himself for the mistakes of the past. It was different to face those feelings, rather than simply running from them. And once he did begin to look at them critically... It had been hard.

But Ariel had been there for him every step of the way.

And things changed radically when she gave birth to their first child.

A daughter.

And it shifted the landscape of his soul.

In much the way Ariel had done the first time he had seen her.

Undeniable love. A love that felt fated in ways he did not ever think he would understand.

But it was actually that love that changed everything for him. That made him fully understand.

A person was never worthy of the love they were given. A person simply had to accept it as a gift, and work to be the best they could.

"She looks so much like you," Ariel said, brushing the top of their daughter's dark downy head with her forefinger.

"And yet, she is her mother's daughter. For she has my heart. Without question. Always."

And then from behind his back he took out the gift that he had brought for her earlier. Not diamonds. Not gold. An orange.

He handed the orange to his wife, and she smiled. "I love you," she said.

"I love you, *ya amar.*"

* * * * *

Caught up in the drama of
Forbidden to the Desert Prince?
Then don't forget to look out for the next
installment in The Royal Desert Legacy duet,
coming soon!

In the meantime, explore these other stories
by Maisey Yates!

Crowned for My Royal Baby
His Majesty's Forbidden Temptation
A Bride for the Lost King
Crowned for His Christmas Baby
The Secret That Shocked Cinderella

Available now!